"I'm out," I say, folding my cards and placing them face down on the table.

We're sitting at the dining room table at the widow Audrey's house. Correction. Audrey, my brother's fiancé.

The wind is howling outside. The wind always howls at nine thousand feet in elevation in the Colorado Rockies just outside of Whiskey Springs where both my brothers now live. With the widow Audrey and her sister Lilah.

"Seriously?" Bradley says. "You're letting Wyatt win again?" Bradley is the oldest of us three brothers and he's the one marrying the widow.

"I can't help it if I always win," Wyatt says. Wyatt is the youngest of us and he's marrying Audrey's sister, Lilah.

It's all one big sloppy mess, if you ask me. But they didn't ask me.

Two brothers engaged to two sisters.

Audrey and Lilah Sinclair. Both nice ladies. No doubt about that. And my brothers are happy. No doubt about that either.

Just not for me.

Audrey comes and sits down in Bradley lap. "Guess what?" she asks, putting her arms around him in an overt display of affection.

"Please tell me it's something good."

"It is." She grins. "Brianna is coming."

"To visit? Finally." Bradley looks at me. "Brianna is their sister."

"That's great news," I say. "I look forward to meeting the elusive third sister."

JUST MELT

THE GRAVITY OF US SERIES

KATHRYN KALEIGH

The Gravity of Us Series

(Reading Order)

Just Breathe

Just Surface

Just Melt

All of the books in the Gravity of Us Series are

standalone and can be read out of order.

However, the books are best when read in order.

ALSO BY KATHRYN KALEIGH

The Gravity of Us Series

(Reading Order)

Just Breathe

Just Surface

Just Melt

Standalone Suspense

Out of Ashes

CONTEMPORARY

Alpine Falls (Maybe Yours) Series

(Reading Order)

Still Yours (Maybe)

Yours for Christmas (Maybe)

Forever Yours (Maybe)

(ALPINE FALLS)

Stranded in Alpine Falls

Belonging in Alpine Falls

The Spirit of Christmas in Alpine Falls

Christmas Wishes in Alpine Falls

Finding True North in Alpine Falls

A Ghost of Christmas Magic in Alpine Falls

Secrets and Second Chances

Honeymoon with a Stranger

Not Our Wedding

(SILVER PINES)

The Way Back to You

Back to Where We Began

When We Were Us

(ONCE UPON FOREVER)

My Forever Guy

Our Forever Love

Forever Vows

Finding Forever

Accidentally Forever

(TRUE NORTH)

Borrowed Until Monday

Still Mine

The Moon and the Stars at Christmas

Perfectly Mismatched

On the Way to Forever

A Merry Little Christmas

On the Way Home to Christmas

It was Always You

(UNBREAK MY HEART)

Begin Again

Love Again

Falling Again

(FOR THE LOVE OF THE FLIGHT)

Just Stay

Just Chance

Just Believe

Just Us

Just Once

Just Happened

Just Maybe

Just Pretend

Just Because

(MAGNETIC NORTH)

Second Chance Kisses

Second Chance Secrets

First Time Charm

Three Broken Rules

Second Chance Destiny

Unexpected Vows

(FALLING FOR CHRISTMAS)

The Heart of Christmas

The Magic of Christmas

In a One Horse Open Sleigh

A Secret Royal Christmas

An Old Fashioned Christmas

(CITY SKYLINE BILLIONAIRES)

Billionaire's Unexpected Landing

Billionaire's Accidental Girlfriend

Billionaire's Fallen Angel

Billionaire's Secret Crush

Billionaire's Barefoot Bride

(TRULY, MADLY, DEEPLY)

The Lady in the Red Dress

On the Edge of Chance

Sealed with a Kiss

Kiss Me at Midnight

The Heart Knows

(STOLEN ECHOES)

When Cupid's Arrow Strikes

Chasing Fireflies

A Chance Encounter

(EDGE OF THE HORIZON)

The Forever Equation

Pretend Boyfriend

All our Tomorrows

Kissing for Keeps

Out of the Blue

The Princess and the Playboy

(RED LIPSTICK KISSES)

Red Lipstick Kisses and Small Town Wishes

Stolen Dances and Big City Chances

Chance Connections and Upside Down Plans

A Christmas Kiss on the Twenty-Fifth

Believe in the Magic of Christmas

Vows of Inheritance Series

(Reading Order)

Vow to Protect

Vow to Redeem

ROMANTASY

(IN THE SPIRIT OF LOVE)

Spirits of the Heart

Out of Dreams and Ashes

Etched Upon the Heart

WESTERN ROMANCE

(LONE STAR HEARTS)

Wanted by a Texas Ranger

Saved by a Texas Ranger

(WHISKEY SPRINGS)

Finding Natalie

Promising Samantha

Falling for Allyson

Saving Savannah

Claiming Charlie

Rescuing Keira

Protecting Gabriella

Courting Isabella

TIME TRAVEL

(INTO THE MIST)

Written in the Wind

Scripted in the Stars

Destined in the Twilight

Promised in the Mist

Trapped in the Melody

(DRAGON'S BLOOD)

Dragon's Blood

Lavender Blue

Champagne Silver

Twilight Frost

Mountbatten Pink

(WHEN HEARTSTRINGS BECKON)

Rescued in Time

Meet me in 1879

(WHEN HEARTSTRINGS ECHO)

Messages Across Time

Falling Through to Forever

Once Upon a Winter's Spell

(BECKONED)

Before the Storm

Twist of Fate

When the Stars Align

Once Upon a Christmas

Once in a Blue Moon

A Wish Upon a Star

(BEGUILED)

When Lightning Strikes

Storm of Time

Midnight Storm

When the Moon Falls

Stormborn Angel

(SPELLED)

Time Tempest

The Heart Remembers

A Moment in Time

Moonlight Shadows

HISTORICAL

(TAPESTRY OF BLUE AND GRAY)

Shadows Beneath Magnolia Blooms

Secrets Among Southern Roses

(IT HAPPENED BY ACCIDENT)

Accidentally Alluring

Accidentally Married

(SOUTHERN BELLE CIVIL WAR)

Beyond Enemy Lines

Love Always

Hearts Under Siege

Hearts Under Fire

Away Down South in Dixie

The Reluctant Bride

Stay with Me

Jasmine Kisses

Magnolia Kisses

Gardenia Kisses

(THE QUINNS)

Wait for Me

Take Me Home

Keep Me Safe

FATED MATES

Riley's Mate

Aiden's Mate

Brayden's Mate

STANDALONE SUSPENSE

JUST MELT

CHAPTER
ONE

Brianna Sinclair
Houston, Texas

I DECLARE A DATING moratorium on the Friday evening after Thanksgiving.

The weather is unseasonably cold for November in Houston.

So cold, in fact, that I'm wearing black tights beneath my beaded little black dress.

Never mix work with pleasure.

Even knowing that, I fell prey to the allure of an older man, an attorney I've been working for for all of a week when he asks me to meet him for drinks after work.

He had such a nice smile. In his thirties, at least ten years older than me, I decide it can't hurt anything.

After all, I spent Thanksgiving alone. By myself. I've never spent Thanksgiving alone.

But my parents are in Atlanta and both my sisters are living in Colorado.

I was invited, of course. Invited to Atlanta and invited to Colorado.

But... work.

I'm sitting in a restaurant I can't afford on my salary as a temp worker, wearing a dress I never should have cut the tags off of. Never cut the tags off a dress that comes with a warning. *No returns once tags are removed.*

There are no qualifications on the tags. No exceptions. Nothing that says you can return the dress if your date doesn't show up. Even if your date asked you to a really expensive restaurant and you went out and bought this really expensive dress to wear to the really expensive restaurant with the handsome, charming boss man who didn't show up.

And there was once an old lady who lived in a shoe.

I glance at the time on my phone. I've been waiting for forty-five minutes.

Forty-five minutes.

Now I have to go. Even if he showed up now, I would look desperate for waiting this long.

The restaurant is crowded with couples and a groups of people coming out for dinner after a day with family.

The tables are covered with crisp white table clothes. Real candles. Live flowers in vases on each table.

Waiters in formal black tuxedos dart silently and efficiently between the tables, seeing to their customers' needs, often before the customers even realize they need anything. Refilling drinks. Sweeping away empty plates. No one notices them. They're simply moving furniture.

Conversations are hushed. No one speaks too loudly or laughs too loud. Not here. Not in this too expensive for working people like me restaurant.

I envy them. Not the formality of it all, but the friends and families. I envy them even though I had chosen not to be with my own family this holiday.

Just like I chose not to be with my family, I'm choosing not to date again.

I've worked in the business world long enough to know that a moratorium needs to have a specified time limit.

Well. I don't have a time limit on my moratorium.

I declare my moratorium to be until further notice. It's my moratorium and if I want it to be until further notice, then it can be until further notice.

I pull a twenty out of my handbag to cover the glass of wine I barely touched and lay it on the table.

No one notices when I get up and slip out of the restaurant.

It's almost like everyone knows I don't belong here. They don't care if I leave. Why would they?

I broke my own rule. I agreed to a date with an employer.

As I wait for the valet to bring my car around. Hand him another twenty I can't afford to spend. I get an email from the temp company that employs me.

With nothing else to do while I wait for my car, I open the email.

Another mistake in a long line of mistakes that are the building blocks of this day.

Dear Ms. Sinclair,

We regret to inform you that we no longer need your services effective immediately.

As you know, we have a zero tolerance policy against employees fraternizing with employers.

My car arrives and I don't even bother to read the rest of the email.

Last time I checked, fraternizing would involve two people. If they think I'm fraternizing, they need to check their sources.

No one showed up.

The man who asked me out must have set me up.

What a champ.

I could respond to the email. Insist that he never showed up. But that is an admission of intent. I have no defense.

Not worth the fight.

Couldn't pay me to talk to him again or to set foot in his office ever again.

Something good comes out of everything.

After I'm in my car, the valet closes my door and I take off.

This is the last Thanksgiving holiday I'll ever spend alone.

In fact, as I drive along the festively decorated streets of Houston, it occurs to me that I no longer have ties to Houston.

My parents are in Atlanta. My sisters in Colorado.

Both of my sisters are engaged to local men, so they won't be moving back to Houston.

It's like adding insult to injury after a long day of disappointments to realize that I no longer belong here.

I've overstayed my welcome.

Without giving myself time to second think myself, I dial my sister Audrey's phone.

CHAPTER

TWO

Caleb Winslow

"I'm out," I say, folding my cards and placing them face down on the table.

We're sitting at the dining room table at the widow Audrey's house. Correction. Audrey, my brother's fiancé.

The wind is howling outside. The wind always howls at nine thousand feet in elevation in the Colorado Rockies just outside of Whiskey Springs where both my brothers now live. With the widow Audrey and her sister Lilah.

"Seriously?" Bradley says. "You're letting Wyatt win again?" Bradley is the oldest of us three brothers and he's the one marrying the widow.

"I can't help it if I always win," Wyatt says. Wyatt is the youngest of us and he's marrying Audrey's sister, Lilah.

It's all one big sloppy mess, if you ask me. But they didn't ask me.

Two brothers engaged to two sisters.

Audrey and Lilah Sinclair. Both nice ladies. No doubt about that. And my brothers are happy. No doubt about that either.

Just not for me.

Audrey comes and sits down in Bradley lap. "Guess what?" she asks, putting her arms around him in an overt display of affection.

"Please tell me it's something good."

"It is." She grins. "Brianna is coming."

"To visit? Finally." Bradley looks at me. "Brianna is their sister."

"That's great news," I say. "I look forward to meeting the elusive third sister."

"We haven't seen her in months," Audrey says.

"What's happened?" Lilah says, pulling off her headset and looking over the back of the oversized sectional.

The first floor of what some call the Albright cabin, others call it the Albright estate due to its large two-story size. The first floor is open with the kitchen, dining room, and living room all spaciously arranged. The second floor has four bedrooms, each with ensuite bathrooms and walk-in closets. Audrey's room has its own spa-like bathroom, two walk-in closets, and a sitting room.

"Brianna is coming," Audrey says.

"Really? When?"

"She's flying up…" Audrey glances at her phone. "Monday."

"Monday," Wyatt looks at me. "Don't you have to be in Denver on Monday for a meeting?"

"I think so." I know so, but I can already sense where this is going.

"You can pick Brianna up at the airport. Save her having to drive up here."

"Yes," Audrey says. "That would be great. Brianna's not the best driver."

"And she always manages to get lost whenever she goes anywhere new," Lilah adds.

Great. Just great. I can already see I'm not getting out of this one.

"I don't know her. I don't even know what she looks like." It's a feeble attempt to get out of it and I know it.

Audrey and Lilah look at each other. "She looks like me with dark hair," Lilah says getting a nod of agreement from Audrey.

"It's time," Bradley says, glancing at the clock on the mantle.

"Yes. We better get going," Wyatt says, pushing back his chair.

"Where are we going?" I ask. Anywhere is better than here with them making plans for me.

"We're going hunting," Wyatt says.

"Oh." I hold up a hand. "I don't think so."

"Come on, Bro," Bradley says. "You don't have to shoot anything. You can do the spotting."

"Gave that up years ago," I say.

"I'll get the guns," Wyatt says, heading to the back door where we keep the guns.

He comes back with two shotguns.

"You're serious," I say. "What am I missing here?"

"It's just bird shot," Wyatt says, handing Audrey a small gun, the size of a pistol, but a type of gun I've never seen before. "But this is for the kill shot."

"You people are starting to scare me," I say.

I grew up around guns. I can shoot. I'm a good shot, actually. Really good. But as an adult, I choose not to hunt.

"This is a VSKP03. An anti-done gun," Audrey says. "We have to use both."

"Wait a minute. You're shooting down someone's drone?"

"If we're lucky."

I glance over at Lilah, sitting with the big dog, a black lab, in front of the fireplace. She is apparently the only one of the bunch who has any sense.

All four of them look at me, then look at each other.

"Yes," Bradley says. "And you are now sworn to secrecy by default."

"Come on Lilah," Audrey says. "You and Wyatt are at the back of the house."

Lilah gets up and follows Wyatt toward the back door.

We all put our coats and scarves on before heading outside.

"Why doesn't Lilah have a gun?" I ask, going with Bradley and Audrey.

"We only have one of these," Audrey says. "And she doesn't like to shoot."

"Well, we have that much in common."

"Stay close to the wall," Bradley says as the three of us step out the front door and line up against the wall.

"I'm really hoping for an explanation."

"You'll get one," Bradley says.

"How do you know there will be a drone?" I ask, my hands in my pockets.

I know it's been awhile since I spent any quality time with my siblings, but this is ridiculous.

Maybe they're just messing with me.

I'm about to call it a night. Just get in my truck and head home.

But then I hear the distinct sound of a bird flapping its wings.

Both Bradley and Audrey lift their respective guns.

"Stay back against the wall," Bradley warns.

The sound of the bird is getting closer. It doesn't sound like any bird I've heard before. It's... louder. With a whirring sound.

Just as the bird sweeps beneath the overhang, Lilah lifts her gun and points it toward the bird. The whirring stops, but the bird keeps going.

That's when Bradley aims and shoots.

The sound of the gun echoes through the night.

I immediately hear the back door slam, then Lilah and Wyatt burst breathlessly out the front door.

The motion lights click on.

"Did you get it?" Wyatt asks.

"Of course."

The bird lies on the ground, just on the other of the porch.

"You said drone," I say, my ears still ringing from the shotgun.

"Bird drone," Wyatt says, stepping out to pick it up.

"Why are we killing bird drones?" I ask. "Please tell me you have a good reason for this."

"Do you remember us talking about someone leaving threatening notes at the door?" Wyatt asks.

"You took care of that."

"It stopped for awhile, but then it started up again." Wyatt takes the bird drone inside and we follow him.

Bradley locks the door behind us, throwing two dead bolts.

Wyatt drops the bird drone on the floor and peels an envelope from its little talons.

"It comes bearing tidings tonight," he says, handing me the note.

"I don't want it."

"Read it."

Giving up on avoiding whatever this is, I take the envelope and pull out a sheet of paper.

"What does it say?" Lilah asks.

"It says *Enjoy your last holiday here. Your days are numbered.*"

"As are his drones," Lilah says with a little scoff.

"Wait a minute. How many of these things have you shot down?"

"This makes four."

"Four drones. Do you know how expensive these things are?"

"Do you know of anyone who would be using them to drop off notes like that?" Bradley asks.

"No. I do not. Isn't this a job for the sheriff?"

"He's an ass hat," Wyatt says.

"It's his job."

"Try telling him that."

Audrey kneels down, digging through the feathers. "Wyatt's friend is tracking down the serial numbers. He'll eventually find out who these things belong to."

"Trent," Wyatt says clarifies. "Trent is helping us."

I rub a hand over my eyes. What the hell has my brothers gotten into now?

"Does Brianna know what she's getting into?" I ask. Do they even understand how serious this could be? Someone is buying expensive drones for what looks like the sole purpose of trying to threaten Audrey and Lilah and possibly now my brothers away.

"No," Audrey says. "We don't want her to worry. We'll explain it when she gets here."

That's got to be a huge mistake. She needs to know. But it's not my decision.

"Okay," I say. "You've gotten me into this. I think you need to back up and tell me the whole story."

Whatever is going on sounds far more serious than they're letting on.

I don't want to be involved, but in a moment of weakness I came up here to spend an evening with my brothers who will no long go anywhere without their women and their dog.

And this where it gets me.

"I need to know everything."

CHAPTER
THREE

Brianna

IN RETROSPECT, I've been preparing for this move for longer than I realized.

I hadn't renewed my lease. Instead, I've been paying month to month and I've been living a minimalistic lifestyle. My condo was furnished, so the furniture isn't even mine to begin with.

It's almost like I've been planning my getaway.

That what it feels like anyway as I board the commercial jet that will take me from Houston to Denver.

I spent the weekend boxing up all my belongings.

Everything that doesn't fit in my two oversized suitcases, got dropped off at the UPS store on the way to the airport.

Done and done.

God help me, I'm putting Houston in my rearview mirror. Didn't think I would ever do that. But these past few months of living here with no family have been just plain lonely.

It was bad enough when my older sister got married and moved out to Katy. It was one of those sudden marriages that made no sense to me. But the guy looked good on paper and the background check I secretly ran on him came out clean.

Turned out, though, that the background check missed some rather important details.

Like the baby he had with another woman before he married my sister.

This probably never would have even come out except that he, Thomas, crashed his private jet and died. All his insurance money went to the baby and the baby's mother. Even the house he'd been living in with my sister was sold out from under her and that money, too went to the child.

But Thomas's grandfather had left a house just outside of a small town in Colorado. Whiskey Springs. He left it specifically to Thomas's wife who just so happened to be Audrey.

The only stipulation was that Audrey live in the house. She doesn't own the house, but she'll live there free and clear, all expenses paid as long as she wants to.

With a one million dollar stipend deposited in her account every year.

I'd been skeptical about the whole thing when it went down, but Audrey had been determined that she had no choice but to go.

She really didn't have a choice. Who wouldn't go? She had to at least try.

Lilah and I tried to go with her, but Audrey wanted to do it on her own. Said she needed to do it herself as part of the process of learning to be single again. That didn't last long.

She'd no more than gotten to the house, not even settled in, when she met Bradley Winslow. They're engaged now.

And not long after that, my other sister, Lilah, got herself in some trouble and went up to live with Audrey in the big house.

Lilah is now engaged to marry Wyatt Winslow.

So my sisters are engaged to brothers.

"Excuse me," I say to a teenage boy with earphones on. "That's my seat."

He stands up and I crawl over into my window seat.

There's a reason I don't fly. It's self-imposed misery. The reason I haven't been to visit my sisters in the six months or so that they've lived in Colorado.

That and driving is out of the question. I rarely even take a day off. How could I possibly drive up there and back? Why would I drive up there and back?

I settle into my seat and watch the baggage handlers toss our luggage from the luggage cart into the cargo hold of the airplane.

It's raining now, so our luggage is getting wet in the process. The only saving grace is that my luggage is hard-sided.

I feel sorry for those people with cloth luggage.

I check my phone. No messages.

Send a quick message to Audrey letting her know I'm on the airplane.

Apparently Bradley and Wyatt have a third brother named Caleb who is supposed to pick me up from the airport and drive me up to Whiskey Springs.

I would have said absolutely no thank you, but I always get lost when I go somewhere new. And from what I'm told, the mountain roads are treacherous, especially since it'll be dark by the time I would be driving up to Audrey's house.

I suppose it's Lilah's house, too, since they're all living there. All four of them. My sisters and their fiancés.

I give myself a few days, maybe a week, and I'll be looking for a place of my own. Need to find myself a job first though. I'm thinking with my experience I can find a job easy enough. Give me a computer and I can do just about anything.

That's the beauty of doing temp work. I learned how to do everything. I can work in any kind of office.

"Fasten your seatbelts, folks, and prepare for takeoff.

We're going to be pushing away shortly and should have you in Denver earlier than expected."

I lean my head back against the seat and close my eyes.

I just want to be there already.

Maybe it's a good thing Caleb is picking me up. No telling where I would end up if left to my own devices. Probably end up in Wyoming or New Mexico.

The airplane starts backing out of its spot and we start driving. I'm beginning to wonder if we're going to drive all the way to Denver when the plane starts racing down the runway and we leave the ground.

Maybe driving, like Lilah had done, wouldn't have been such a bad idea, I decide as I grip the edge of the seat.

For the next few hours, it's just me and my teenage seat mate lost in his own world, headphones over his ears.

Maybe he has the right idea.

Me? I keep reminding myself.

Life changes come with strife.

If life changes were easy, everybody would do it.

CHAPTER
FOUR

Caleb

As INSTRUCTED, I get to the Denver airport, park, and find my way to the luggage carousels.

I'm on time. A little bit early, actually, but the plane, it seems, must have arrived earlier than scheduled.

Passengers are frantically grabbing their luggage, as they always do at airports, and heading out of the terminal, meeting me head on. I dodge them. A lot of families traveling together this time of year. A few businesspeople wearing their business suits.

I fit in with the businesspeople. I look like just another businessman wearing a business suit, except I'm going the wrong direction and I'm not here for myself. I'm just here to pick someone up.

The things we do for family.

Speaking of family, my brothers have gotten themselves tangled up in some kind of mess revolving around the widow Audrey.

From what I was told, she inherited the house from her late husband's grandfather, the only stipulation being that she has to live in the house. She can't not live there and she can't sell it.

Oh. And every year she gets a million dollars deposited in her account.

Not a bad deal.

And apparently someone else knows about this arrangement. Someone who wants her out.

Someone wants her out so they can move in.

So far their tactics have been leaving threatening notes at the door. Messages, they learned after some time, left by bird drones.

One of their tactics, however, was not harmless. They kidnapped Bradley's dog, Biscuit.

As far as I'm concerned, that was taking it too far.

Biscuit was unharmed, returned unscathed a few hours after he was taken from their house, right while everyone was upstairs working on installing shelving in the closets.

Whoever was able to get into the house to get the dog, without being recorded on their cameras, had installed their own scrambler *inside* the house.

Since no more incidents like kidnapping the dog have occurred, whoever did it must know that his scrambler has been disabled. Very likely since he had cameras planted inside Audrey's house.

Cameras that they pulled down and stored out in the tool shed.

Me? I would have pulled them out and put them down the garbage disposal or tossed them in the river. But they're keeping them for evidence even though they won't go to the sheriff with this thing.

Bradley went to the sheriff when it started, but the sheriff blew him off. Now they've decided to take things into their own hands by shooting down the guy's drones.

It seems like a dangerous game to me.

I'm not sure they see the danger.

If someone will mess with a pet, he'll mess with a person.

Something needs to be done. I don't know what it is, but I know there has to be something.

A young lady who absolutely does look like Lilah with long dark hair grabs at a black hard sided suitcase from the conveyor belt. She wobbles on high heels and the suitcase continues its path on the belt.

She's wearing a charcoal gray pencil skirt and matching jacket with an emerald green blouse peeking out beneath it.

I instantly know she's Brianna Sinclair. There is no mistaking her resemblance to Audrey and Lilah.

I cover the distance in three long strides and, stepping to her right, drag the suitcase off the belt.

"This one, too?" I ask, nodding toward the matching one coming along behind it.

"Yes," she says, watching with dismay as it rolls past her.

I grab it, too, dragging it off the moving conveyor belt.

"Thank you so much," she says, pushing her hair back. "I missed them the first time around."

"I can see why. They weigh a ton."

She looks at me with a little bemused smile.

She looks like her sisters, but she's so much prettier. At first I think it's her bow-shaped plush lips with the little smile. But, no, it's something in her eyes. So deep and such an unusual shade of teal green. Looking into her eyes, I see so much wisdom. This is not a shallow girl. This is a woman with depth. The kind of woman a man could hold a deep philosophical conversation with.

"I'm Caleb Winslow," I say.

"Brianna." She holds out a hand. Even with three-inch heels, the top of her head only comes to my shoulder.

My gaze never leaving hers, I put my hand in hers.

A connection shoots through me and for a moment I forget where we are. I forget why I'm here. Hell, I'm not even sure I remember my own name.

"I guess you're my ride then," she says.

"I guess I am." I reluctantly let go of her hand and take the two handles of her suitcases.

She moves to pick up the leather computer bag sitting at her feet.

"Let me get that," I say.

She smiles. "I'm so glad you're here," she says. "I don't know how I would have gotten this out to the rental car place."

"Your flight must have been early," I say, noticing that there are only a couple of other people at the luggage conveyor belt.

"It was. The pilot was no nonsense."

"Did you fly first class?" I ask as we make our way along the concourse.

"What? No. But it wasn't bad. The teenager sitting next to me just sat quietly and listened to music the whole time."

"Good. You never know what you're going to get on these commercial flights."

She looks at me with questions she doesn't ask.

"You hungry?" I ask.

"A little. Yes."

"Me too. If you're not in a hurry, we should stop for food before we head up into the mountains."

"Okay." We step outside and she pauses.

"What's wrong?"

"Nothing. It's just. Cooler than I expected."

"Your sisters didn't warn you about the weather?"

"They did. It's just. I don't even own a coat."

"How do you not own a coat?" I ask.

"Houston." She shrugs.

Houston. A quick reminder that she's only here to visit. And she's practically related to me with both my brothers engaged to her sisters.

I pull myself together.

It's not like I haven't seen pretty girls before.

CHAPTER
FIVE

Brianna

Caleb Winslow is much more handsome in person than he was in the photo Audrey sent me. And no one warned me that he's a gentleman.

It's such a relief to have someone to help with my luggage. I honestly hadn't given much thought to how I was going to handle it when I'd packed.

All I'd been thinking about was just how much I wanted to get out of Houston.

One slip up and it was like I suddenly had a vile taste in my mouth for the city.

Honestly, though, I think it had been building up.

Maybe I'd sort of self-sabotaged myself. That or I had simply gotten so lonely so I just wanted to spend one evening with an interesting man who found me attractive.

Caleb is nothing like what I expected.

The photos my sisters had sent me of Wyatt and Bradley always were with them wearing flannel shirts and work boots. So that's what I had expected of Caleb.

After all, he lives in the same small town and runs their family business.

But instead of a flannel shirt, he's wearing a business suit. Since I'd worn office work clothes by habit, he and I actually look like we could be colleagues. I hardly even know how to wear anything else.

His car also surprises me. He drives a new Lexus SUV. I had expected him to drive a truck. Somebody, Lilah maybe, had mentioned that the brothers all drive trucks. Maybe that's just for work. And since this isn't work...

After loading my luggage in the back, he opens the passenger door and holds it while I climb inside.

Then he goes around and climbs into the driver's seat.

"I hope this wasn't too far out of your way," I say.

"Not at all," he says, turning on the heater. "I was in Denver for a business meeting today."

"Right. Well. I appreciate the ride."

"I don't mind. It's no trouble. Besides, we can't have you getting lost up in the mountains."

"My sisters told you I get lost easily." I look out the

window at the mountains in the distance. "Is that where's we're heading?" I ask.

"It is. We have a bit of a drive. There's a sandwich shop I usually stop at. Sound okay?"

"It sounds good to me. Anything is fine."

"That's what we'll do then."

His definition of a sandwich shop is slightly different from mine.

My definition of a sandwich shop is literally grabbing a sandwich and chips to go.

Caleb's idea of a sandwich shop is what I call a pizza place. A sit down restaurant.

If he doesn't mind taking the time to eat, then I don't mind either. It's not like I'm in any hurry now that I'm here and on my way to Whiskey Springs.

We order our food and find a table near the window to wait.

"Do you come into Denver for business often?" I ask.

"About once a week or so. Not for the family cabin and timber business though. I have some... what most people would call side hustles... of my own."

"Side hustles. I'm a fan of side hustles."

"Oh? You have one?"

"No. Not at the moment. But I've given it a lot of thought."

"Somebody told me you do temp work."

"That's right. I'm actually a paralegal, but I like learning different things. You can put me in any office anywhere and I can do the job."

"That's impressive."

I can almost see him thinking. Wondering if I'd be a good fit working for him.

"But what I want to do is to translate that into working for myself," I say before he can get any ideas.

"It's the only way to be successful. To be really successful."

"Are you really successful?" I ask.

"I'm getting there."

"How do you do it? How do you run your family business and do your side hustle at the same time?"

"My two brothers do all the hard work. I just make sure the work gets done. And our mother is the office manager."

"That's efficient."

"It is actually."

One of the servers brings out our sandwiches.

"This is good," I say after one bite of the cheesy sandwich.

"Stick with me, Kid," he says. "I won't steer you wrong."

Something about the way he says it has a delicious little shiver running along my spine.

I believe him.

There's something about Caleb that garners my confidence.

As I eat, I study him beneath my lashes.

Clean-shaven. A strong jaw. A metro haircut. He looks

like he could be from Houston. A businessman from Houston. Easily.

But then there's something different about him, too.

Mesmerizing blue eyes. Eyes the color of a stormy sea.

Those stormy eyes go well with the passion I sense coiling just below his serene surface. So calm on the exterior, but there's more to this man than meets the eye.

He's not the typical businessman I work with. And there's something about the way he looks at me that has my blood thrumming through my veins.

It's going to be a long ride up to Whiskey Springs.

CHAPTER

SIX

Caleb

We've no more than gotten back in my SUV and headed out of the city when I get a call from Bradley.

The Denver highways, as always, are crowded. There is no time of day when Denver highways have a lull that make it easy to get around. The city outgrew its structure years ago.

"And I thought Houston traffic was bad," Brianna says. "Is it always like this?"

"Pretty much. My brother is calling." I push the answer button on my steering wheel. "Hey Bradley. You're on speaker with Brianna."

"Hi Brianna."

"Hi Bradley."

"Something up?" I glance over at Brianna. The poor girl is walking into a mess and she has no idea about what she's getting into. None.

"Yeah. Something's happened." He hesitates and I almost take him off speaker. "We just got a call. Claire's house is on fire."

"Wait. What?"

Claire is Audrey's housekeeper. She's been taking care of the Albright house, now Audrey's house, for as long as I can remember.

"Is she okay?"

"Yeah. She just so happened to be here today. And she brought her cat with her."

"Thank God."

"Yeah. We're all going to pile in the trucks and drive over there. See if anything can be salvaged."

"Taking the dog?" I ask, knowing they can't leave him home by himself. Not after what someone kidnapped the dog.

I want to warn him that this could be a ploy to get them out of the house, but I can't say too much without having to explain it Brianna. She doesn't know yet and it's not my place to be the one to tell her.

"Of course. "We're taking the dog and the cat."

"Good deal. So I've got Brianna. If I get there before you get back, I'll..." I glance over at her.

"Just drop me off at the house," Brianna says. "Audrey can send me the code."

"Okay," I say. "I'll do that."

And I'm counting on them being back. I'd rather not leave Brianna there at the house alone.

We end the call.

"From what I've heard, Claire's had a really hard time lately," Brianna says.

"I guess she has," I say. Still not committing to much because I don't know what Brianna knows about Claire.

"She was in the hospital, right?"

"Right. I think she slipped down."

"That's what Lilah told me. She didn't say much else about it."

"So," I say, determined to change the subject. "How long are you planning on staying?"

"Oh." She sweeps her hair out of her face. "I don't think I'm going back to Houston."

"Ever?"

"No. My parents are in Atlanta and my sisters are here. I'm thinking I'll find a place of my own in Whiskey Springs."

"It's a whole lot different from Houston," I say. "It might take you a minute to get used to the small town."

"My sisters like it. I think I'll be okay."

And then there were three.

That's all I can think.

Somehow all three Sinclair sisters have found their way to Whiskey Springs.

I refuse to be like my brothers.

I refuse to fall for one of the Sinclair sisters.

No matter how hot she happens to be.

CHAPTER
SEVEN

Brianna

THE RIDE from the restaurant up to Whiskey Springs isn't nearly as bad as I had imagined it would be when I agreed to riding with a stranger.

Caleb is pleasant and entertaining. He tells me trivia about the area as we drive into the mountains. Tells me about the "Great Flood of '2010" that closed the roads to Whiskey Springs for six months while they rebuilt them. How he had been devastated because he missed out on summer camp.

"I never had the opportunity to go to summer camp," I tell him.

"Seriously? Going to summer camp every year played a significant role in making me who I am today."

"I did some summer college classes between my junior and senior years of high school. That was about it."

"What did you do all summer?"

"We spent some time with our grandparents. Went swimming. Watched television. Played games."

"A life of leisure."

"Surely you had some free time during the summers."

"We did. Our Grandpa took us boys hunting, but never together. Said it was too dangerous to keep up with three boys all carrying guns at the same time."

"Sounds like a very smart man." I look out the window as we cross a bridge over a mountain stream full of rocks and boulders. Nothing in any way like the rivers back home.

"In case you're wondering," he says. "Hunting did not stick with me. I haven't been hunting since I was sixteen."

"Why not?" I shift my attention over to look at him. He doesn't look like the kind of guy who would hunt. But still. He is from the small town.

"I don't know. I guess I couldn't see the point of killing for sport."

"I don't either. That's what stores are for."

"Exactly. And they could leave kitchens out of houses, too."

"That's what restaurants are for," I say.

"Exactly."

"It's like washing your own car."

"Or doing your own taxes."

In that moment, I feel a connection with Caleb. A real connection. One I haven't felt in a really long time.

Over something so simple as a shared understanding that people really don't need kitchens in their houses.

No one else in my family ever understood that concept. They believed in making home-cooked meals. But me? To me cooking at home was right up there with trying to sew your own clothes.

In Caleb I've met a kindred spirit.

It's getting dark now and he concentrates on driving. The roads are more narrow now. The curves shorter. And we're climbing higher into the hills.

In the darkness I can't see much. But I can see enough to know that we're moving into what is not only beautiful, but dangerous country.

A little like Caleb himself.

Beautiful but dangerous.

CHAPTER
EIGHT

Caleb

W\ESTOP for a short restroom break on the east side of Whiskey Springs, giving Brianna her first look at the small town.

"Is everything decorated?" she asks once we're back in the car and I drive slowly along Main Street.

"Pretty much. They have a saying around here. 'If Christmas was a town, it would be Whiskey Springs.'"

"That's a good saying. And it fits."

"We take pride in our Christmas festivities. Every Christmas Eve, there's a masquerade ball at the Whiskey Springs Lodge."

"There's a lodge," she says.

"A very nice one." I almost tell her I'll take her there, but I catch myself. "I'm not even sure your sisters have been. You should all go."

"I'll ask them about it," she says.

I turn off the main highway and start the climb up toward the widow... toward the Sinclair house. Might was well start thinking about the house as the Sinclair house and not the Albright house. And while I'm at it, I should think of Audrey as Audrey. Not the widow.

"The road up near the house is treacherous," I tell her. "Very narrow with steep cliffs. Nothing between the car and the edge of the cliff. If the weather is bad or even just foggy, I suggest you avoid it at all costs."

"Thanks for the heads up. Has anyone ever gone over the side?"

"There have been tales."

She shivers. "But not anyone you know personally?"

"The old man Albright is the only man who lived there for years and he was mostly a recluse."

I have to give her credit for not looking afraid as we drive across what I call the narrows. The area I spoke of with the severe drop off. She merely looks curious.

"The house is right up ahead," I say. "They must be home." There are lights on in the house.

But as I pull up in front of the house, I see that there may be lights on, but their trucks aren't there. Claire's car is parked there and so is the sheriff's truck.

"What's the police doing here?" Brianna asks.

"I don't know."

I pull up in front of the house and put the SUV in park, leaving the motor running.

Sheriff Morgan is sitting in his truck.

"Wait here," I say. "I'll find out what he's doing."

"Okay."

The sheriff rolls down his window as I walk up to his truck.

"Sheriff," I say.

"Evening Caleb."

"Something wrong?"

"Just checking things out. Making sure there are no problems."

"What kind of problems?"

"With Claire's house burning down and all."

I put my hands on my hips and look back over at the big house, lit up now with motion sensor lights. "Not seeing the connection."

"I'm sure you heard they had some trouble out here," the sheriff explains.

"That was a long time ago," I say. "In the summer."

"Just doing my job."

"See anything suspicious?" I ask, keeping my voice calm, but I'm feel tension coiling beneath the surface.

"Everything looks okay."

"Well then. I'm going to get Brianna settled inside."

I swear the man's eyebrows lift off his head. I've never

seen much reaction from the sheriff, but he has a visible reaction to Brianna's name.

"So the other sister finally made it up here," he says.

I'm wishing I hadn't told him Brianna's name. Not much I can do about it now.

"I think we've got this," I say.

"Going to just sit here and make a phone call before I head out," he says, picking up his phone.

"Alright then," I say. Not much I can do if the sheriff wants to sit outside the house and make a phone call.

I go around to the passenger side and open Brianna's door. "You have the code, right?" I ask.

"Yes. What does he want?"

"Nothing. Just wants to sit there."

I walk around to the back of the SUV and pull out her luggage.

"Strange?" she asks.

"A little. But he's the sheriff."

"Okay," she says. "I guess I should feel safe with him sitting outside." She glances over at his truck.

"I'll stay with you until they get back."

"You don't have to do that. They'll be back soon and you've done far more than you signed up for."

I grab her computer bag from the back seat, toss it over my shoulder, and heft her luggage up onto the porch.

I watch behind her, looking toward the sheriff's truck, thinking about the bird drone they'd shot down a few days ago, while Brianna keys in the code to the door lock.

It shouldn't be unsettling having the sheriff in front of the house. It seems like it should be comforting, all things being equal.

Wyatt called the guy an ass hat. Maybe I should have explored that a bit more with my brother. To find out if there's something specific he doesn't like about Sheriff Morgan or if it's just a general dislike. I never had much (any) dealings with the sheriff myself. I'm a law-abiding citizen and keep my nose clean.

The door opens right up for Brianna and she steps inside the dark house. I automatically reach for the light switch on the wall, taking in a quick scan of the room, before I roll her two suitcases inside.

I leave her leather computer bag on the kitchen island next to a vase with white roses.

The vase of roses wasn't there last Friday night when I'd been here.

Lilah and Wyatt are building a flower shop and green-house here on the property not far from the house, but it's taking them longer than they expected to get it off the ground.

As such, I'm curious where they got the flowers, but not my business.

"I can just wait here until they get back," I say again.

She runs a hand through her hair. "I'm just going to change clothes, wash my face, then sit here." She sweeps a hand behind her toward the sectional. "Maybe take a little nap before they get back."

"Okay," I say. I can't very well insist that I stay here when she's telling me to leave.

Audrey doesn't want Brianna to know about the stalker until she tells her.

And besides, the sheriff is right outside.

What can possibly go wrong?

"Thanks again for giving me a ride up," she says with a little smile that I find endearing.

"I enjoyed the company," I say. "Well. You have my number, right?"

"Yes. Lilah sent it to me."

"If you need anything at all… if you get frightened up here… just call me. I'll come right back."

"I'm not afraid," she says. "I'm sure, everything considered, I'll see you soon."

I smile. "Yes. I have no doubt about that."

"Walk me out," I say. "And lock the door behind me. I think there are deadbolts."

"I'm okay," she says. "The police is right outside. I don't think anyone is going to break in."

"You're right. It's just… it's a new place." I should so tell her to be wary.

But my phone chimes with a text from Bradley letting me know they've left Claire's house and are on their way back.

"They're on their way back," I tell Brianna. "So I'll say goodnight."

"Goodnight."

She follows me to the door and I stand on the porch and wait, listening until she clicks all the deadbolts into place.

My hands in my pockets, I walk over to my car, ignoring the sheriff and climb inside.

I think my brother Wyatt is onto something. Something doesn't sit right with me about Sheriff Morgan. I can't put my finger on it, but it's there. Maybe he's just, like Wyatt said, an ass hat.

Thinking about that as I put the car in drive and head down the mountainside makes me smile to myself.

Or maybe it's not really thinking about the sheriff being an ass hat.

Maybe it's thinking about Brianna.

What is it about these Sinclair women that us Winslow boys find so damned attractive anyway?

CHAPTER
NINE

Brianna

I TAKE a minute to look around the first floor of the house, but with the FaceTime calls I've shared with my sisters, I feel like I know the house well enough.

What I didn't know, however, from the videos was just how clean it smells. Claire, the housekeeper, was there today and she left the house smelling like outdoors, specifically like the fresh scent of spruce trees.

Not even trying to haul my suitcases upstairs, I open one of them up, rummage around for some sweatpants and a sweatshirt, some sneakers, and head upstairs to the empty bedroom.

Four bedrooms and only one of them is unoccupied. I'm a little surprised that Wyatt hasn't moved in with Lilah, but right now he has his own bedroom.

I get changed, hanging my business clothes in the empty closet, newly designed by Audrey, and empty hangers waiting. Then I wash my face, pull my hair back, and head downstairs with a book in hand.

I curl up on the sectional in front of the banked fireplace and wonder if I can figure out how to start a fire.

I'd just decided that I need to leave it alone for now when someone knocks on the door. I hadn't heard anyone drive up and I hadn't seen any headlights coming through the closed window shades.

It's not my sisters because it's their house. They wouldn't knock.

Annoyed more than anything else at being disturbed, I get up and walk over to the door.

"Who is it?" I ask. This might be a remote cabin outside a small town, but I'm from the city. I don't just open the door because someone knocks.

"Sheriff Morgan."

Of course. I hesitate. There's probably some kind of penalty for not opening the door to the sheriff. If television is any indication, he might just knock the door down and come inside anyway.

I unlock the top deadbolt first. Then the second one.

Then I unlock the door itself and pull it open.

The sheriff is standing there, in his full uniform, thumbs

in his belt loops, sunglasses, at night no less, and he's chewing gum.

I don't like to make quick judgements on people, but I have an instant inexplicable dislike for him. I honestly attribute the dislike to the sunglasses. Not a big fan to begin with. But a law officer shouldn't come to someone's door at night wearing sunglasses. It's just creepy.

"Everything okay in here?" he asks.

"Everything is great. What do you need?" I realize, a little too late, that I should probably curb my tongue before I make an enemy of the small town sheriff before I'm even introduced, but he just smiles.

"I've heard a lot about you and I wanted to introduce myself."

I lean against the door. "I'm Brianna Sinclair," I say, hoping that will satisfy him. "Audrey and Lilah's sister."

"Uh huh." Chewing gun. Creeping me out with the sunglasses.

"So," I say. "They aren't home. Maybe you can come back when they're home."

"If you don't mind, I'd like to come in and take a look around."

"Why?" I give up on trying to keep the annoyance out of my voice.

"There was a report."

"Of what?"

"Step aside, ma'am. I'll be out of your way in no time."

I have no choice. Not knowing what this police officer

will do if I don't comply, I'm not inclined to find out. I step away from the door, letting him saunter inside.

"I've always liked this place," he says.

I step back, watching him. Not saying anything.

He walks over to the kitchen, leans over and sniffs one of the flowers.

"What kind of report?" I ask.

"Excuse me?" he turns and looks at me. He seems to have completely forgotten why he's here.

"You said there was a report."

"Right," he says. "Probably just kids." He slides his sunglasses off then and I immediately change my mind about not liking them.

I liked him better with sunglasses. As he peers at me with piercing brown eyes. I cross my arms and take a step back.

"How long are you planning on staying?" he asks, with a quick glance over at my luggage standing at the bottom of the stairs.

"I haven't decided yet." Not his business if I have.

"Well. The winters around here are what most call unforgiving."

"What are you saying?"

"I'm saying that a city girl like you isn't likely to enjoy being up here in the mountains in the winter. Summer maybe. But not winter. It's much too... unpredictable."

"I'm sure I'll be fine." How dare he warn me away like this?

He takes another step toward me and I'm feeling decidedly uncomfortable now.

I don't know this man and I don't know what he'll do.

I move over to the couch and pick up my cell phone. Hold it front of me like a shield. I don't know what I'm going to do with it. I don't know who I'm going to call, but I feel better with it in my hand.

I don't know how far out from here my sisters are. It probably doesn't make any sense to call them.

But Caleb can't be too far away. He did tell me to call if I need anything.

Then I see headlights shining through the window shades.

Relief washes through me.

My sisters are home and they'll have their boyfriends with them.

This sheriff can take up whatever bug is up his ass up with them. I want nothing to do with him.

Narrowing his eyes, he looks toward the door.

I give him a little smirk.

He points his sunglasses at me. "You've got an attitude." There is no humor in his tone.

I shrug.

Someone knocks on the door.

"Come in," I call out, leaving no uncertainty that I want whoever is here to come inside. Please. Anyone.

Caleb pushes the door open and take in the room, looking at me, then the sheriff.

"What's going on?" he asks me, but he's looking at the sheriff.

I shake my head.

"There was a report," the sheriff says.

Caleb looks at me. "Did you make a report?"

"No," I say, shaking my head again.

"Sheriff Morgan." Caleb crosses his arms across his chest. "What can we do for you?"

"Just paying a friendly visit," he says. "Following up on a disturbance report."

"Who made a report?" Caleb asks.

"Came in anonymous," he says. "Probably just kids."

"Probably," Caleb says. "We'll call you if we need anything."

"I'll leave you to it then." Sheriff Morgan slides his sunglasses back on his face and heads to the door.

Caleb looks at me, then follows the sheriff.

As soon as the sheriff is outside, Caleb locks the door.

I drop onto the sectional.

"What was he doing here?" Caleb asks.

"I don't know. He just showed up at the door. Insisted on coming inside. I had to let him in, right? He's a policeman."

"I guess," Caleb says.

"How did you know to come back?"

"I pulled over at the cabin just down the way to wait for him. When he didn't leave, I came back."

"I'm glad you did. He sort of creeped me out."

We listen as the sheriff drives off and just as he's leaving two more sets of headlights come this way.

"That's Wyatt and Bradley," Caleb says.

"I hope so," I say, leaning back on the sofa, more than content to let Caleb take over from here.

Audrey steps in through the door first, along with Biscuit pulling on his leash, Bradley right behind her.

"What's going on?" she asks. "We just passed the sheriff leaving."

I get up and meet Audrey halfway across the room, sweeping her into a big hug.

"It's so good to see you," I say. "Let me look at you."

Lilah comes inside, rushing straight over to give me a hug, too.

"I missed you so much," Lilah says.

My eyes are misting over with happiness at seeing my sisters for the first time in months.

Wyatt comes in next, an older woman with him, and lets the door slam closed behind him.

"What was that ass hat doing up here?" Wyatt asks.

Caleb and I look at each other.

"I was hoping you would know," Caleb tells Wyatt.

"Where did those flowers come from?" Lilah asks, seeing the vase of white roses on the kitchen island.

Audrey walks slowly toward them, then stops. Looks at me. "Did you bring these?" she asks.

"There were there when we got here," I say.

"I think you need to tell her," Caleb says.

"Tell me what?"

"Everything," Audrey says, turning back to me.

I sit down again. I have a bad feeling about this.

"I'll just be upstairs, settling in," the older woman says.

"Brianna, this is Claire," Bradley says. "She's going to be staying with us for awhile.

"Hello Claire," I say. "I'm so sorry about your house." The damage must be bad enough that she needs to stay here.

"It's okay." She holds the pet carrier close to her. "I have what's important. The rest doesn't matter."

TEN

Caleb

I SIT down next to Brianna and listen while Audrey and Lilah go through the story about how someone has been threatening them since Audrey arrived here at the house last summer.

I hadn't known about the flowers that had appeared in the house shortly after Audrey arrived. They still didn't have an explanation for how they had gotten inside the house.

As for the vase of white roses on the counter, Wyatt takes it out the back door and leaves them there.

"They could have bugs," he says, seeing us all looking at him when he gets back inside.

"Bugs?" Brianna asks.

"Wyatt's friend swept the house for bugs... cameras... and found nearly a dozen."

"What's going on here?" Brianna asks. "You should have told me."

"We didn't want you to worry," Lilah says.

"You should be worried. Have you reported this to the police?"

"That was the police," Caleb says. "The man who just left."

I make a face. I don't know what to say about that.

"He's an ass hat," Wyatt says, sitting down next to Lilah.

"Surely there's someone else to report this to," Brianna says.

"We decided to figure out who's doing it on our own," Bradley says.

"I'm not sure that's a good idea," Brianna says.

"Agreed," I say. My brothers just look at me. "What? I do. I don't think shooting down someone's drones is the answer."

Brianna looks at me. "Drones?"

"They've been shooting down someone's bird drones," I tell her.

"What's a bird drone?" Brianna asks me.

"It's a drone disguised as a bird. Someone has been

dropping threatening notes off with the drone. It took them a long time to figure out how someone was dropping notes off at the door without getting caught."

"Who would have thought to notice a bird flying past?" Audrey adds. "It was quite ingenious."

"How did you figure it out?" Brianna asks.

"Wyatt and Lilah figured it out," Bradley says.

"Actually it was Wyatt," Lilah says.

He takes her hand. "I share the credit."

Brianna and I exchange a glance. It seems like our siblings aren't taking this nearly as seriously as it warrants.

Maybe they've been part of it for so long that they can't see it anymore.

"I need to go up and help Claire move my things to Lilah's room," Wyatt says.

"Not to change the subject, but what's the status of Claire's house?" I ask.

"Burned to the ground," Wyatt says softly as he stands up. "Audrey and Lilah decided she should live with us for the time being."

Just like Bradley and then Wyatt moved in temporarily.

"Seems like you're going to need to add on some extra rooms," I say.

Audrey and Bradley look at each other and I can see from their expressions that I just inadvertently provided them with the solution to a problem they'd been work-ing on.

"Well," Wyatt says. "In the meantime I'm going to be sleeping on the chair in Lilah's room."

Right. I admire him for protecting Lilah's reputation, but we're all family here. There's no need to pretend.

"Can I talk to you for a minute?" Bradley asks me.

"Sure."

"Let's just get our coats and take Biscuit for his walk."

"My coat's in the car," I tell him. "I can get it."

"We're got extras. Come on."

Biscuit, hearing his name, gets up and does a full body shake, then barks once.

As we're heading out, a black cat comes down the stairs and jumps up on the kitchen island like he knows right where he's going.

The Sinclair house or whatever name they decide it goes by, is getting more than a little crowded.

CHAPTER
ELEVEN

Brianna

SITTING ON THE SECTIONAL, I watch all the activity around me.

This is nothing like what I expected to be walking into.

Wyatt is upstairs, moving his things into Lilah's room so the housekeeper can have a room of her own. They don't seem to mind making him moving into her bedroom official. But it's not for me to say.

Lilah has been through a lot herself. When she moved up here to Whiskey Springs, she'd been getting as far away from an ex-boyfriend as she could.

After an altercation that involved her tossing the contents of a glass of wine into a woman's face at the

Hobby Center where she was working as a hostess, she was fired. It didn't matter that the woman, Beatrice, had started it. That she had been taunting Lilah. Lilah was the one who had tossed the wine.

I'd been with Lilah the night all that had happened. I'd seen just how devastated she was. She vowed that she was giving up bartending, a promise to herself she had stuck to. She'd also vowed that she wasn't going to date again. That promise to herself didn't seem to have stuck.

A lot of what she'd been afraid of was the two-year statute of limitations for the woman, Beatrice, to file charges against her for tossing wine in her face.

But either way, Lilah looks happy now. Wyatt knows what happened. I might have been a long way away in miles, but the three of us are close and we share most of what happens.

I guess that's why I'm surprised they didn't tell me about the bird drones and how the stalker is still leaving threatening notes.

Lilah is feeding the cat on the kitchen island and Audrey is acting like it's the most normal thing in the world.

With Bradley and Caleb outside, Wyatt upstairs, it's just me and Audrey sitting on the sectional.

"How are you?" I ask.

"I'm good," Audrey says. She looks good. I don't see any signs of the strain that were there a few months ago after her husband had died in a plane crash. Like Lilah, she looks happy.

"And you?" she asks. "What do you think about our guys?"

"I've hardly had time to get to know them, but my first impressions are good. You two certainly look happy."

"What about Caleb?" she asks.

"What about him?"

She shrugs. "Just curious to know what you think about him. He doesn't come around very often, so Lilah and I don't know him very well. You probably spent longer with him driving up here than we've spent with him altogether."

"Well. He seems like a nice guy. Likeable." He definitely won points with me when he came back to rescue me from Sheriff Morgan. I hope what I felt from the sheriff was my imagination, but it certainly hadn't felt like it at the time.

"Have you met Sheriff Morgan?" I ask.

"Yes." Audrey scrunches up her face in distaste. "Unfortunately."

"Then it wasn't just me."

"What? You met him?"

"Oh yes. He came inside the house. He totally creeped me out. Caleb came back and the guy finally left."

"What did he do?" Audrey pulls a throw pillow into her lap and holds it there.

"It's hard to explain. It's like he was looking around. And he was asking me personal questions like how long I'm planning on staying here. And telling me how I won't like the winters up here."

"Wyatt calls him an ass hat."

"I know. It's rather fitting, isn't it?"

"He's actually the one who came and told us about Claire's house. And he came back here?"

"I guess so. He was here when we drove up."

Lilah, finished feeding the cat, comes over and flops down on the sofa.

"You know what would be funny," she says. "If you started dating Caleb and we all lived here together."

"Lilah," Audrey says with a warning in her tone.

"No," I say. "That would not be funny, Lilah."

"He is kind of cute, right Audrey. And he's a businessperson, like you, Brianna."

I sweep a hand down my sweatpants. "Not such a businessperson right now, am I?"

"Whatever. You know what I mean."

"I'm going to forget you said that," I say, glancing toward the back door where Caleb is out there right now with Bradley.

And even though I said I was going to forget she said it, I know perfectly well that *actually* forgetting about it isn't going to be nearly so easy to do.

Because she's right. Caleb is a handsome man. And, yes, I noticed his stormy sea blue eyes. But. No. Not interested.

Definitely not interested in getting caught up in whatever it is my sisters have going on here.

CHAPTER
TWELVE

Caleb

AFTER I PUT on an old coat Bradley tosses in my direction at the back door, we follow Biscuit around while he makes his rounds about the back yard. Apparently he has a very specific route he follows and he never goes past the shadows of the trees.

"You always keep him on a leash now?" I ask. "Doesn't look like he wants to run off."

"Absolutely. He doesn't get any alone time either. Not since he was dognapped."

"Yeah. Somebody crossed a line when they did that."

"You can say that again. You don't want to be around when I find out who took my dog."

"Actually I kind of do. I want to see you kick that person's ass. Because if you don't, then I'll have to do it."

"Have to get in line behind Wyatt and the girls."

I look back toward the house. All the lights are on, but all the shades are also down. Bradley and Audrey had installed motorized shades on all the windows so that no one could stand outside after dark and watch them inside the house.

The motion light at the back door clicks off, but there's plenty of moonlight to guide our way. Not that Biscuit needs light at all. He knows his route by heart.

"This old house is filling up," I say.

"You've got that right. Not what I expected to happen. But having Lilah here makes Audrey happy."

"You don't mind it then? Not really? And now the housekeeper lives with you."

"That's just temporary."

"Right. Just like you were going to live here temporarily."

"That's different," he says.

Biscuit finds the place that suits him and throws leaves everywhere like he's frantically digging for treasure.

"What did you want to talk to me about?"

"Just wondered what you thought about Brianna. We're all just meeting her."

"She's smart," I say. "I get the impression she can do anything she sets her mind to."

"Sounds like the other sisters."

"And she's fiercely independent. More so than either Lilah or Audrey."

"I get that vibe from her, too."

"I don't think you have to worry about her living here in the house for long," I say. "I think as soon as she finds a place of her own, she'll be moving out. As soon as she finds a job."

"Huh. Not really what I was asking. If having here making Audrey happy, then I'll deal with it. Biscuit's finally ready to head back inside."

The dog takes off at a run toward the house. Bradley gives him full rein, but the dog stops just before he reaches the point that it snaps back.

"How does he do that?" I ask. The motion light clicks on as Biscuit hits its range.

"I don't know. I'm surrounded by people who are smarter than me."

I scoff. "First of all that's decidedly not true. And second, Biscuit is not people."

"Try telling that to him." The dog is sitting at the back door, waiting for us to come along and open it for him.

"I wouldn't mind knowing what's up with that sheriff," I say before we reach the door.

"What do you mean?" He opens the door and lets

Biscuit run inside by himself, leaving the two of us alone on the back porch.

"He was hanging around outside when we got here. So after I left Brianna here, I stopped at your old cabin just down the way and waited for him to drive past. When he didn't, I came back. He was inside the house. Standing there looking at Brianna."

"Looking at her how?"

"I don't know, but Wyatt's right. There is something seriously wrong with that guy."

"I thought it was just me. That's why we don't tell him anything."

"You think he knows who's doing it?"

"I don't know what he knows," Bradley says. "But I do know that I don't like him being around here."

"Agreed."

"It's freezing out here," he says. "Let's get back inside. Get a fire going in the fireplace."

"Thought you'd never say that."

"Here," he says, stepping toward the stack of cut firewood. "Make yourself useful."

He proceeds to pile firewood in my arms. Not the least bit concerned that I happen to be wearing a designer suit beneath this old coat.

THIRTEEN

Brianna

BISCUIT RUNS in the back door, by himself, still wearing his leash, and lays down in front of the fireplace.

"Three went out. One comes back. Should we be concerned?" I ask.

"Nah. They're just outside. Talking."

As though on cue, the back door opens and Caleb walks in behind Bradley. Both of them have their arms loaded down with firewood.

Bradley carrying firewood looks perfectly natural.

But seeing Caleb carrying an armload of firewood, especially while he's wearing what I know to be a designer suit beneath the old coat, makes it hard for me to look away.

It just says so much to me about him. Here's a man who basically has his own business in addition to running his family business, wearing designer suits, and looks like a Houstonian. But at the moment, he's wearing an old coat that obviously doesn't belong to him and he's carrying an armload of firewood.

Those two things together exemplify everything I know about him so far. He's successful and yet he puts his family first. That's what I'm seeing from watching him stand there while Bradley unloads the firewood from his arms.

He must sense me looking at him because he looks over and smiles.

I look away quickly, feeling like I've been busted studying the man who's been nothing but kind to me.

My face feels a bit heated as I look down at my phone, pretending to be suddenly engrossed in its blank screen.

"Want a beer?" Bradley asks, dusting his hands on his jeans after unloading all the firewood.

"Sure," Caleb says.

"Anybody else?" Bradley asks.

My sisters and I shake our heads.

Wyatt comes back down the stairs. "All done," he says. "Anybody want a beer?"

"Great minds," Caleb says, sitting down beside me.

I try not to read too much into him sitting next to me. Where else would he sit? He knows that Bradley is going to sit next to Audrey and Wyatt is going to sit next to Lilah. Unless he sits on the hearth or on the chair off to itself, next to me is that only place left.

Bradley and Wyatt come back with beers, handing one to Caleb. He just holds it, not drinking it.

I pick up my bottle of water and drink, trying not to look at him.

"Is Claire okay?" I ask Wyatt.

"She's settling into her room. We stopped at the General Store on the way back and bought her some basics to get her through the next couple of days. She's a very strong woman. Very resilient. Insists that as long as she has her cat, nothing else matters."

"I can't even imagine going through something like that," Audrey says. "And not being upset about it."

"She's upset," Lilah says. "She has to be. But she's been through so much lately. It's probably just one more thing to have to deal with on top of everything else."

The black cat, Claire's cat, hops onto the back of the sectional and climbs into Lilah's lap. "Why aren't you up there with your mother?" Lilah asks, but she buries her face in his fur.

"What's a typical day like around here?" I ask during the moment of silence while Bradley gets a fire going. "Shooting down bird drones. Houses burning down. Creepy sheriffs coming into the house?"

They all just look at me for a moment. Audrey and Lilah. Caleb. Wyatt. And Bradley.

Then they all laugh.

"Welcome to Whiskey Springs," Audrey says. "Where there's never a dull moment."

Great. Walking into a hornet's nest is exactly what I wanted to do.

But for them, it seems to be their new normal.

"Bad timing on my part," I says. "Showing up on the same day that Claire needs a place to stay. I could have shared a room with Lilah."

"It's okay," Lilah says, squeezing Wyatt's hand. "Wyatt's been sleeping in the chair in my room anyway." She looks more serious than she has since I got here. "After what happened with Biscuit, we sleep in our rooms with our doors locked. Just to be safe."

I look at Caleb then. I don't know why. I guess I just wonder what he thinks about all this. Like me, he's not really a part of it.

And somehow that makes me feel like he and I are kindred spirits.

I hadn't realized just how much I needed that feeling of connection with someone.

And it just so happens that he's the one I'm getting that feeling from.

Not my fault.

CHAPTER

FOURTEEN

Caleb

WITH THE FIRE crackling in the fireplace, Biscuit snoring softly, and the cat, aptly named Blackie, I listen to the conversations flowing around me.

Two conversations at once, sometimes connecting, sometimes not.

Audrey and Bradley talking about the possibility of adding onto the house.

Lilah wondering if there's any kind of stipulation in the trust about that.

Lilah and Wyatt talking about the greenhouse and flower shop they're trying to get off the ground. Apparently they had some kind of setback that kept them from moving as quickly as they had hoped.

Audrey suggesting they wait until spring, which neither one of them want to do.

"It's going to start snowing any day now," Bradley says. "And you'll be forced to wait whether you want to or not."

"That's why we need the greenhouse up and running so we can have flowers growing over the winter."

"If you're not ready to start selling, won't they just be lost?" I ask.

"Well, yes," Lilah says. "But they'll be practice flowers. This is all new to us."

"I guess that makes sense," I say, taking a sip of the beer I'm not going to drink. Not when I have to drive down the mountainside. In the dark.

"It can't hurt," Wyatt says. "We have to learn how to put together arrangements."

"That," I say. "Would be so far over my head, I can't even begin to imagine."

"Anybody can learn anything they want to learn," Lilah says.

I lift my beer to her. "I like your optimism," I say.

"If anybody can do it," Brianna says. "Lilah can." She looks at her sister. "Have you been getting any painting done? I haven't heard you say anything about it lately."

"A little. When the weather's warm enough, Wyatt and I walk down to the river's edge and I paint. I'm also doing some sketching."

"I'd like to see," Brianna says.

"Okay. I'll show you tomorrow."

I'm getting the impression that Brianna is highly protective of her siblings, especially Lilah, the youngest.

"I didn't know you painted," I say to Lilah.

"She's very good," Wyatt says. "And I'm not just saying that because I like her."

Lilah shoves at Wyatt, but he just wraps his arms around her, holding her close.

Brianna obviously knows that Lilah is artistic and wants to encourage her.

"I'd like to see some of your work, too," I say. "It's nice to have someone artistic in the family."

Lilah looks up at Wyatt with questions. He just shakes his head.

There's something they aren't telling us. Audrey and Bradley are officially engaged, but I'm getting the sense that Wyatt and Lilah have talked about getting married, too. Privately.

"Well, I've got to drive home," I say. "And I've got to go to work tomorrow. So I'm going to say goodnight."

"Give me that beer," Wyatt says. "And I'll walk you out."

After I hand the beer over to Wyatt, I glance over at Brianna who's studying me again with those intense teal green eyes of hers. Eyes that seem to see everything. Even things people don't necessarily want her to see.

"I'll be seeing you soon," I say in what sounds like a general statement, but I know it's directed at Brianna.

I love my brothers, but Brianna is the one here that I find interesting.

And as much as I do not want to get involved in whatever they have going on here... this Sinclair-Winslow connection, I already know that I want to see her again.

No getting around that.

Maybe I'm just curious about her.

She and I have a lot in common and I'm curious about what she thinks about all this chaos surrounding our family and I'm curious about what she's going to do now that she's here.

Wyatt follows me as I step outside onto the porch. Pulls the door closed.

"Tomorrow we're all going out to search for a Christmas tree to chop down. You in?"

My plans for tomorrow flash through my head. After spending today in Denver and then tonight here, I have lots of catch up on and I don't have a lot of flexibility in my day.

I can't keep getting behind.

"Sure," I say. "What time?"

"Lunch."

"Is it a surprise?"

"Just didn't want to put you on the spot."

"On the spot?"

"You know. With Brianna. Don't want to make any assumptions."

"Okay. I see." I clasp him on the shoulder. "Thanks for

inviting me. Trying to be more involved in family things. So. I'll be here."

As I head to my car, I wonder just how much more it is than that.

Doesn't matter though. Not really.

I was planning on being involved more with my family anyway.

And now that I know about all the threats they're getting, they could use my presence.

It has nothing to do with Brianna.

Not one single thing.

I smile to myself as I climb into my truck.

CHAPTER

FIFTEEN

Brianna

SHORTLY AFTER CALEB LEAVES, I head up to my room.

I ignore, as best I can, the odd sense of loss I feel as he drives off. It's not like me to feel that way.

Bradley carries my luggage upstairs, but I don't unpack yet. There's plenty of time for that.

Instead I change into my pajamas and wonder what it is about Caleb that I find so intriguing.

I've avoided dating for a very long time because I work all the time and work is the only place I ever meet people.

Since my company has...had... no longer my company... a very strict policy against dating those we work with...

even if the guy doesn't even show up for the date... I just avoided dating.

If I had met Caleb under different circumstances, I might have allowed myself to look at him with the possibility of dating him.

Even though my family doesn't a policy against dating people in the family (obviously), I could date him if I wanted to.

But. It's just too weird.

Too interconnected.

And I'm too well-schooled in not mixing things. Dating Caleb would be too much like mixing family with... well... family.

I'm too tired to try to understand it right now. I just need to get some sleep and everything will look better in the morning.

After getting changed into my pajamas, I walk over to the door and throw the lock.

Something has to be done about living this way.

Living in house where we don't feel safe doesn't seem like a very good way to live.

I understand Audrey being determined to stay here in the house.

This house is the only thing she inherited from her late husband. The house and the million dollar annual stipend that she gets along with it.

That's nothing to sneeze at. And, yes, I'm pretty sure I'd fight to stay here, too.

And on top of that, she's got Bradley behind her.

From what I've gathered through various conversations, the Winslows have money of their own so the money isn't their motivation for wanting to weather all this to be with my sisters.

They seem to genuinely care about my sisters and my sisters are definitely smitten with their men.

I stand at the window and look outside. I have to raise the window shade to look out, but I refuse to hide behind it.

With the lights out, it's not like anyone can see inside anyway.

I stand there and look across the meadow, across the valley, at the tall, rugged mountain peaks capped with forever-snow glowing in the moonlight.

It's beautiful here. And if I raise the window just a fraction, I smell the fresh scent of the spruce trees outside. It's so refreshing and so clean, it almost hurts to breathe it in.

Despite all the chaos going on, with the threatening notes and the bird drones and the creepy ass sheriff, I can see the beauty of this place. It's the kind of place a person could get used to.

Our parents raised us girls in Houston, only moving back to Atlanta after we were grown and out of the house to care for their elderly parents, so I've always been a city girl.

Is it so easy, then, with just one day, to turn a city girl into a small-town mountain girl?

I have plenty of time to figure all that out. Plenty of time of experience the small town. The winter that I've been told I won't survive.

Thinking back over that conversation with the sheriff, makes me bristle and makes me feel all the more determined to stay here at least through the winter. Just to prove the ass hat wrong.

He doesn't know me. He's just trying to frighten me away.

The thought makes me pause.

But why? Why would the sheriff care who lives in Audrey's house? What stake could he possibly have in our lives?

I shake off the notion and turn away from the window. I leave the shade up just out of spite.

Just to show whoever might be out there watching my window that I'm not going to cower behind window coverings. If someone wants to watch me sleep, if they find a way to see into my second-floor window, then more power to them. Let them be bored out of their minds.

I have nothing to hide.

I climb into bed, click on my reading light, and open up my book.

I've barely read more than two short paragraphs when I find my attention wandering back to Caleb. Wondering what he's doing tonight. Wondering how he spends his time when he's not working.

I shake my head.

Not my business.

I should not be thinking about him. My thoughts are being very bad for distracting me into thinking about Caleb Winslow.

Not for me.

Definitely not for me.

I'm not in the market.

This Winslow-Sinclair thing is far too complex.

CHAPTER

SIXTEEN

Caleb

THE NEXT MORNING I get as much work done as I can. I'd prioritized everything in my head last night, so I take care of what has to be done first. The rest can wait.

There has to be some kind of perk to owning my own business even if it is getting spend time with my family.

About eleven o'clock, I drive home from the office and change into blue jeans and a sweatshirt layered over a t-shirt. I put on my hiking boots.

It's been a while since I went out in the woods for any reason and going out to hunt down a Christmas tree seems like a good excuse to get myself outside again.

I'm enjoying getting to know my brothers' girlfriends.

And maybe I'm looking forward to seeing Brianna again.

It's not such a bad thing. She's going to be part of my family now anyway.

Since it's a dreary day and looks like snow, even though it's not in the forecast, I take my truck.

I mostly drive my truck around Whiskey Springs and take the car when I'm driving into Denver.

I toss an axe into the truck bed just in case, even though I'm certain my brothers will have everything they need for chopping down a tree.

Even though Wyatt is the designated lumberjack of the family, we're all proficient at using an axe and a chainsaw. About half our business is trees and firewood and the other half is cabin rentals.

It all goes hand in hand and we can all do whatever needs to be done in any part of the business, having learning everything from the ground up as children. A rite of passage. Our after school activities consisted of chopping wood and following our father out on maintenance calls.

I pull up to Audrey's house and feel a twinge of unexpected nostalgia at the sight of smoke drifting out of the chimney.

My brothers have something I don't have. They have a home life.

As they should.

They deserve to be happy.

I could have a home life if I wanted to.

I just never found the person I wanted to commit to spending the rest of my life with.

And that includes sporadically looking with intention—if dating apps are included in that definition.

I can safely say that I have had no luck in my romantic search endeavors whether by accident or intent.

Sure. I could have settled. There are plenty of women in Whiskey Springs who consider any one of the Winslow boys a good catch.

Maybe that's why I refused to date anyone who knows my family.

Being someone's good catch is not my idea of dating. To me that's sort of like going hunting by baiting elk.

As I step out of my truck and walk up to the front door, I find myself looking around for anything suspicious.

I hate that. I hate it for my brothers and their girl-friends. Having to be on edge all the time is no way to live.

I'll do whatever I can to make that go away.

Bradley opens the door as I step up onto the front porch.

"Just in time," he says. "We're about to have lunch."

"Good." I step inside the warmth of the living room and take off my coat.

I look around. Claire is there, doing something in the kitchen along with Audrey. Lilah is sitting at the computer at the kitchen table, stacks of different colored index cards all around her. Wyatt is banking the fire in the hearth in preparation for leaving the house.

But I don't see Brianna.

Maybe she's decided she doesn't want to go with us.

Wyatt had given me a heads up in case I didn't want to feel like I was being set up with her. Maybe someone had done the same thing for Brianna and she had chosen to stay home.

I'm rather surprised that they will let her stay home alone while everyone else is out hunting for a tree, but then maybe Claire is staying behind, too.

Deciding that makes sense, however disappointing it might be, I sit down at the kitchen table.

"Can I help you with anything?" I ask Lilah.

"No. I'm just adding a few flowers to my list."

"So this is how you do it?" I ask.

"Pretty much," she says with a little shrug.

I'd like to know more. I'm intrigued that she can learn anything she sets her mind to, but before I can ask her anything else, a movement at the top of the stairs catches my attention.

It's Brianna. Anything I was thinking about involving index cards and flowers and learning vanishes out of my head.

All I can see is Brianna.

CHAPTER
SEVENTEEN

Brianna

While Audrey and Claire make lunch, I dash upstairs to grab a cashmere scarf I remembered packing in one of my suitcases.

I'm getting the feeling that Audrey likes having Claire here. I have to admit it's not bad having a live-in house-keeper. We certainly didn't have that growing up, but things change.

I'm also getting the impression that Audrey likes having a house full of family. That part rather reminds me of when we were growing up, but this is better because we're the adults now and for my sisters, at least, they have their boyfriends.

They're happy. I can see it all over their faces.

And today we're going out in the woods to chop down a Christmas tree.

A new tradition, Audrey is calling it.

We had a fake tree growing up. It was nice. Festive and elegant all rolled into one, but it wasn't real. I had a boyfriend who always had a real tree in their home and I envied him. Their house always smelled like Christmas. It was a scent I never forgot and it could take me back to my teenage years in a heartbeat.

Even after I moved out on my own and could have gotten a real tree, I didn't, because well... it was just me and I didn't see the point.

But now with all of us together, it seems like the perfect thing to do.

The only thing missing is a boyfriend for me.

Of course, since I don't have a boyfriend, it's a little difficult to imagine how that piece might fit into the puzzle.

But... I can't help but think about Caleb. Maybe it's because I'd spent so many hours with him yesterday. It was quite honestly the closest thing to a date I've had in a very long time. At least the closest thing to a date where the guy actually showed up.

But it's not something I should be thinking about.

I'm sure he has better things to do than traipse about in the woods with us looking for a Christmas tree. How many people does it take to find and chop down a Christmas tree anyway?

Halfway down the stairs, I stop, my boot clad feet frozen to the wooden step, one hand on the railing.

Sitting at the kitchen table, looking right at me with stormy sea blue eyes is Caleb.

I was just thinking about him and here he is. Looking at me with a slightly amused expression.

My heart slams into my throat.

It's almost like I conjured him up by thinking about him.

It takes me a second before I realize I'm grinning.

Pulling my gaze away and looking straight ahead, I wipe the grin off my face as best I can, not very well, I'm sure, and continue my way down the stairs.

I walk over to the dining table where he's sitting. It would be rude to do otherwise and put my hands on the back of the nearest chair.

"Hi."

"Hi." He smiles at me with something in his eyes that has drunken butterflies flying about in my stomach.

"I didn't expect you to be here today," I say.

"I could hardly turn down the chance to find the perfect Christmas tree to bring home."

Home. I bite my lip.

I sense Lilah watching me out of the corner of my eye, but right now I don't care.

"They say it's a new tradition," I say.

"I guess what's old is new."

I look at him, my head tilted sideways. So going out to chop a Christmas tree is nothing new to Caleb.

And yet... he's here.

"Okay," Audrey says, bringing a platter piled high with sandwiches over to the table. Bradley behind her with two bags of potato chips. "Sandwiches and chips for everyone. Lilah, Dear, can we borrow your table?"

"Sure," Lilah says, closing her computer and putting it on the counter behind her.

I notice that no one touches her index cards or even offers to. Apparently it hadn't taken long for everyone to learn that Lilah doesn't like her things messed with.

She has a system that works for her and works well.

No one questions that.

"Have a seat," Caleb says, pulling out the heavy chair I'm standing behind.

I sit down next to him.

As everyone takes a seat and the platter of sandwiches makes its way around, I wonder just why no one bothered to tell me that Caleb was coming today.

Maybe they hadn't known.

Or maybe they hadn't thought it was worth mentioning.

The fact that I think it was worth mentioning tells me something. I need to be careful.

This Sinclair-Winslow connection thing just might be contagious.

CHAPTER

EIGHTEEN

Caleb

COMING today had been a good idea.

A very good idea.

One look at Brianna across the room, her standing on the stairs, her eyes locked onto mine, and I know I'd made the right decision.

She was caught off-guard. I have no doubt about that. No one had told her I was coming. I like that. I like having the element of surprise on my side.

Brianna Sinclair is a vexed brunette elfin princess.

As beautiful as she is, she always wears a slightly vexed

expression. As though she's thinking and thinking thoughts that only she can think.

I get the sense that her thoughts are so more complex than anyone else, they don't even begin to compare.

I don't know much about her sisters to compare her to them, but I do know that Lilah is a genius at learning things.

Audrey, I don't know what her super power is yet.

But Brianna. Brianna is just plain brilliant.

Nothing gets past her.

I listen to the conversation swirling around us.

Bradley is trying to tell Audrey which trees make the best Christmas trees.

"Definitely the blue spruce," he says.

"According to what I researched," Lilah says, jumping into the conversation. "The Douglas and Frasier fir trees are actually best. The Douglas fir is one of the top-selling Christmas tree varieties. It has soft, sweet scented needles and a full form. The Frasier fir is durable and has a strong scent."

"Her mind is like an encyclopedia," Bradley says.

"Tell her something once and she'll remember it forever," Wyatt says affectionately.

"Scary, isn't it?" Audrey says.

Even as the conversation swirls, I'm focused on Brianna. She smells like a mix of lavender and vanilla.

She watches the others while she eats, not saying anything.

She's like a guardian, watching over her sisters. Waiting for someone to make a misstep. I would not want to be the one who made the mistake of stepping out of bounds with one of her siblings.

"What kind of tree do you think is best?" she asks, turning to me.

"The blue spruce," I say, then add a nod toward Lilah. "No offense. But it's what we sell."

"Your tree farm," Brianna says.

"Yes. People flock from the whole state to buy our trees."

"The whole state?" she asks with one eyebrow raised in amusement.

"Maybe not the whole state. But definitely all around."

"It could be the whole state," she says.

"What do you mean?"

"With the right marketing, you could go national."

No one says anything for a few minutes. I get the vague impression that everyone is watching us with interest.

"I think your father tried that once, didn't he?" Claire asks.

"That was before our time," Bradley says. "Things were different then. It might be worth checking into."

"We would just need a good website," Audrey says.

"Oh," Lilah says, leaning forward. "We could do guided virtual tours and people could pick out their own trees."

"Then you just have to figure out the logistics of shipping," Brianna says.

My brothers and I all three lean back in our chairs and look at each other.

We don't have to say a word to know what we're all thinking.

These Sinclair women are freaking amazing.

They're amazing individually, but together, they're unstoppable.

It's an amazing thing to witness.

As I sit there eating my sandwich, I realize it's already too late for me.

I'm hooked.

Brianna

AFTER LUNCH, we all meet up at the back door to put on our coats.

Since I don't have a coat, I'm instructed to just choose one from the rack of half a dozen coats left over after everyone grabs theirs.

It appears to me that all the coats are men's coats and are much too big.

"Try this one," Caleb says, pulling a red faded coat from the rack.

He holds up what looks like a well-worn wool coat. A lady's coat.

"Okay. It's smaller than the other ones," I say.

"I don't know how it ended up here. No idea at all, but it looks like the coat my grandmother used to wear."

"Really?" I slide my arms into the sleeves while he holds the coat. "How did that happen?"

"I guess one of my brothers must have brought some coats from our parents' house." He begins buttoning me into the coat. "I have a feeling you're not the only southern girl who arrived without a coat."

I can't say why, but him buttoning my coat is truly one of the sweetest things anyone has ever done for me.

"A perfect fit," he says after I'm all buttoned in.

I look up at him as he adjusts my scarf around my hair.

His gaze snags on mine and I practically forget to breathe.

His stormy blue eyes look into mine with such an intensity that I can't quite wrap my head around.

"Alright," Bradley says. "Everybody bundled up? It's going to be cold out there."

"I think we're all good," Caleb says just before he slides a wool cap onto my head, down over my ears.

I scowl at him, knowing this can't possibly be a flattering look for me.

He just shrugs and a quick glance around tells me that everyone else is wearing similar wool hats. Definitely not flattering. But apparently a necessary evil.

"Are you sure you're going to be okay here by yourself?" Wyatt asks Claire.

"I'll be okay," Claire says, patting the phone in her pocket. "One cross vibe and I'll have you on the phone."

"I feel better about leaving the house with you here," Audrey says, giving the older woman a quick hug.

"Go have fun," Claire says. "I'll have everything ready for the tree when you get back. Just like we talked about."

With Biscuit leading the way, we all head out, wind slapping the cold air into our faces the minute we're outside. Now I see why Caleb tucked my hair beneath the scarf. Otherwise it would have been all in my face.

Bradley holds a chain saw in one hand at his side and Wyatt carries an axe easily across one shoulder. Caleb, unlike his brothers who look like they mean business, has no weapon. He looks like he's just out for a stroll.

Audrey and Bradley, hand in hand, lead the way, urging Biscuit out of his usual route and heading along a path that leads into the trees.

Lilah and Wyatt, also walking hand in hand, follow along after them. Lilah gazes at everything, doubtless with her artist's eyes.

Caleb and I are left to bring up the rear. Unlike the others, we are not walking hand in hand.

In fact, it seems so strange and strikingly obvious to me, that I shove my hands in the pockets of my coat... Caleb's grandmother's coat.

We follow along a trail that takes us alongside the rushing river, so loud it's almost impossible to hear each other talking.

As we veer away from the river, I glance over at Caleb.

"Do we have a particular destination in mind?" I ask.

"I'm sure Bradley already scoped out some trees."

"If you have a tree farm, why don't we just go there and find one?"

"Because that would be too easy," Caleb says. "This way, you all get the whole experience."

"I see. So it's about the experience. But I don't see how it's different from going to your tree farm for the whole experience."

"Has anyone ever told you that you're too smart for your own good?" he asks.

I smile over at him. "I might have heard variations of that before, but never as a compliment."

"It's definitely a compliment," he says. "Do you need me to kick anyone's ass for you?"

"Sounds like you're just itching for a fight."

"Maybe you bring out the knight-in-shining armor in me."

"In that case, I'll let you know," I say.

As we follow the trail, leading downhill, it becomes less easy to walk. A bit more rugged and, for me, as a city girl, more treacherous.

My boot slips on a loose rock and before I can do more than put up a hand to catch my balance, Caleb is there grabbing hold of my arm to keep me steady.

"Be careful there, City Girl," he says.

I look over at him sideways. He just smiles and takes my hand, squeezing it palm to palm.

Something. A new awareness. Shimmers through me.

With the cold hitting me from the outside and the warmth flooding me from within, I'm overwhelmed with feeling.

A bluebird flies across the trail in front of us and the sun comes out, casting a glittery glow to the air.

I feel a lightness in my step that I can't remember feeling since... well... since forever.

In this moment, fleeting though it may be, all is right with my world.

CHAPTER
TWENTY

Caleb

WE REACH A MEADOW FULL OF, imagine it, blue spruce trees.

Now that I have Brianna's hand in mine, I don't want to let go. Ever.

It's an odd sensation, watching her wearing my grandmother's wool coat.

Even though it felt like we'd walked downhill, we've reached a meadow with a light layer of snow on the ground.

The high country.

Brianna stops and looks around. "It's beautiful here," she says with obvious awe.

"It is, isn't it?" I follow her gaze.

"Have you been up here before?"

"I'm sure I have. My brothers and I have been all over these mountains at one point or another."

"You were just free to roam?"

"Pretty much."

"It seems treacherous beneath its beauty. Making it deceptive."

"It'd say that's accurate."

"Are we supposed to be looking for a tree?" she asks, lightly touching one of the

"Yes." I'm looking at a blue spruce tree off to our right. Doing a mental height gauge. Decide it's too tall for inside the house.

Brianna steps around the tree I'm looking at, and since I'm still holding her hand, I follow.

We walk around a tree not more than five feet tall.

"Nice tree," I say.

She looks at me with her teal green eyes. "Are we allowed to cut here? Who's land is this?"

"It's Audrey's land," I say, a little impressed that she would ask that question. "She can cut whatever tree she wants to cut."

She looks at me with a perplexed expression, like she doesn't quite believe me, but Lilah calls out, interrupting whatever she was thinking.

"Come look," Lilah says. "We found the perfect tree."

Brianna takes one last longing look at the tree in front of us. "I guess the search is over," she says.

"Go ahead," I say, letting go of her hand. "I'll be right there."

As she walks off, I pull a red streamer out of my coat pocket and tie it around one of the limbs of the tree.

Then I catch up to her just as she reaches the others.

"You don't think it's too tall?" I ask her.

"Not if we cut off the bottom," Wyatt says.

I nod my approval. Not at the tree. I couldn't care less about which tree they decide on. But he has my approval at supporting his girl's choice.

I already know that Brianna will get behind whatever Lilah chooses.

"Is this the one we're getting?" Bradley asks Audrey.

"Looks like it," Audrey says.

"Okay, Kids, stand back. This could get messy."

I herd the ladies, along with Biscuit, back away, out of range of the tree, while Wyatt stays next to Bradley, holding the trunk of the tree, getting ready to make sure it falls in the direction they want it to.

It's a big enough tree that it's going to easily reach the ceiling of the house.

The chain saw echoes through the air, disrupting what was a serene vista. Biscuit paws at the ground and barks, tugging at his leash, not liking the disruptive noise.

I wonder how long it's been since a chain saw has been heard out here. If ever.

The tree crashes to the ground with a loud thud, landing in exactly the spot it was supposed to.

Bradley turns off the chainsaw and the quietness returns leaving just the memory of its loudness lingering on the air.

Now it's time for us to wrap the tree up to protect its limbs and carry it back to the house.

"Time for me to go to work," I tell Brianna before I leave her with her sisters to help my brothers.

The fun part of the trip is over.

CHAPTER
TWENTY-ONE

Brianna

We walk ahead of the guys on the trip back to the house.

The guys walk behind us, the three of them carrying the tree.

Personally, I think it's going to be too tall for the house, but Lilah picked it out and as the youngest sister, she pretty much gets what she wants.

If it was me, I would have picked out the little tree I'd found. It was the perfect height with perfectly formed limbs. I console myself with the knowledge my perfect tree gets to live another year. Maybe next year. Maybe next year, it'll be my turn to pick out the tree.

"This was fun, wasn't it?" Lilah asked as we make our way back toward the house.

"It was," Audrey says. "Our new tradition."

"It just seems so normal," Lilah says. "We don't get a lot of normal around here."

I see now why Caleb asked if he needed to kick someone's ass. I feel like asking that very question right now.

Not that I would or could if I wanted to. I've never been in a fight my whole life. The closest any one of us has ever been to being in a fight was when Lilah tossed the contents of a wine glass into someone's face.

We're a pretty tame bunch, all in all.

I get the sense that the Winslow brothers can't say the same thing about themselves.

They're good guys, but no one is going to mess with them. Especially not when they're together.

They make a formidable team, the three of them.

Formidable and handsome. My sisters have done well for themselves and I'm maybe a tad bit envious. My sisters chatter about nothing and everything as we walk back toward the house. Their noses are red from the cold, but they're both smiling.

Secure and happy in their relationships.

As we round a curve in the path, I look back over my shoulder toward the guys following close behind us. They, too, are talking animatedly among themselves. I can't hear their words, but they sound happy, too.

Caleb catches me looking back and grins at me. I grin back before I catch myself. Grinning back at him is like a spontaneous reaction. I can't control it. Even if I wanted to.

Looking forward again, my heart skitters with lightness.

I can almost imagine what it might be like if Caleb and I were together.

Maybe it wouldn't be so bad. Three sisters and three brothers.

Rather old-fashioned.

People in Houston would probably have a field day about the whole thing.

I can hear them now.

She couldn't go and find a man of her own.

She just hooked up with the brother of her sisters' boyfriends.

It's like one of those old black and white westerns.

Caleb laughs at something someone says.

Who cares what other people think.

If they met the Winslow brothers... if they met Caleb, they would understand.

And even if they don't understand, it's not their business.

"We should go on a sleigh ride," Audrey says.

"A sleigh ride?"

"Yeah. You know. With horses. It could be another one of our traditions."

Maybe my imaginary acquaintances in Houston aren't

so very wrong. Maybe being up here in Colorado is like being in a different world. Maybe even a different century.

Looking over at Lilah, I shrug. I guess we'll be finding some horses. And a sleigh.

As long as Caleb is part of this activity, I won't mind. In fact, it might be a little bit fun.

TWENTY-TWO

Caleb

"I told you this tree was going to be too tall," I say as we lower the tree down on its side to assess whether to cut some more off the bottom or maybe off the top.

"If we cut some more off the bottom," Wyatt says. "We'll have to cut off some of the bottom limbs, too."

Bradley stands back with his hands behind his head. "That would work. It would still be proportional that way."

"Let's take it outside. Again." Wyatt puts his coat back on.

Bradley and I do the same.

The girls are sitting in front of the fireplace with a fire that looks dangerously high for the fireplace, but no one seems to be worried about it.

With the tree back outside, we lay it extended out across the steps and Bradley picks up the chainsaw.

Wyatt and I hold the tree steady while he cuts off a good six inches, then some of the lower branches.

"Lilah wants to keep these branches," Wyatt says, stacking them up on the porch.

"What for?" Bradley asks, taking a broom and sweeping the saw dust off the trunk of the tree.

"I think she wants to use them to make garland or something," Wyatt says.

"Good idea," Bradley says.

I watch my brothers with amusement. The both of them are so far domesticatedly gone, it's just funny. Two grown men stacking tree limbs and sweeping off the trunk of a Christmas tree before they take it back inside.

"What are you smirking about?" Wyatt asks.

I hold up my hands. "I didn't say a word."

"Didn't have to," Wyatt says. "I can see it written all over your face."

"I don't know what you're talking about. I think it's cute. The two of you living in domesticated bliss."

"Jealous," Bradley says.

"Yep."

"Just give him a minute. He'll catch up."

"I can just go," I say. "If you two want to continue this conversation without me. Since you seem to have forgotten that I'm standing right here."

"You're not going anywhere," Bradley says.

"Once you fall under the spell of a Sinclair woman, there's nothing you can do but ride it out," Wyatt says.

"From what I hear," I say. "You fell under that spell in about two seconds."

"I don't think it was that long," Bradley says, looking at Wyatt. "Do you think it was that long?"

"Nah," Wyatt says. "It was more like instantaneous combustion."

"At least he admits it," Bradley says. "Most men wouldn't have the nerve."

"Let's get this tree back inside," Wyatt says. "It's going to be a perfect fit this time."

We carry the tree back inside, wrangle it back into the tree stand, then get it standing up again. And, as predicted, this time it fits perfectly. Just enough room at the top to put whatever decoration the girls decide they want up there.

"We're having hot chocolate," Audrey says walked past us toward the kitchen. "Anybody want any?"

Bradley and Wyatt do, of course. When I don't say anything, they look at me.

"Sure," I say. "Why not?"

I glance over toward the sectional where Brianna and Lilah are sitting to find Brianna looking right at me.

Her eyes widen and I smile.

She looks away, but not before she smiles back.

I might be protesting this whole domesticated thing, but Brianna is making it difficult to do so.

All she has to do is look at me with those big teal green eyes and I forget whatever it is I'm protesting.

TWENTY-THREE

Brianna

I'm sitting with Audrey in front of the fireplace, flames burning entirely too high, sorting through stacks of decorations. She has multi-colored lights. Clear lights. Big old-fashioned lights, that oddly enough, are brand new in the box.

"Did you get a little carried away with the lights?" I ask.

"I couldn't decide which ones would look good on the tree."

Lilah holds up a strand of the big old-fashioned looking lights. "These," she says. "Definitely these."

"I agree," I say. "You can wrap the smaller twinkly ones along the banister."

"And around the fireplace with some of those tree branches they're cutting off," Lilah adds.

"We should have hot chocolate," Audrey decides as the men come back inside after making another adjustment to the height of the tree. "Want hot chocolate?"

"Sure," Lilah and I both say.

Audrey heads over to the kitchen to heat water.

"You two are really in the festive spirit," I say.

Lilah reaches over and puts a hand on my arm. "Don't look so vexed. It's good to see Audrey so happy."

"Yes. It is. And you, too."

Lilah smiles and wraps her arms around herself. "I keep hoping I don't wake up just to find out that it's a dream."

"It's not a dream, Lilah. It's a life you're making for yourself."

"I'm so glad you're here."

My gaze strays toward Caleb. He looks so at ease with his brothers. "Me too," I say.

Lilah leans forward and whispers.

"You think he's cute," she says.

"We're not twelve," I say, wiping the grin off my face and replacing it with my usual vexed expression.

"Too bad," she says. "I think he likes you."

"How do you know that?" I ask, my gaze straying involuntarily straying back to Caleb.

Lilah rolls her eyes. "I can tell. Anyone can see it."

"You're imagining things," I say.

"Why would I do that?" Lilah asks, looking vexed herself now. "That would take entirely too much effort and there would be no point."

I look over at her.

"I didn't mean it like that," I say.

"I know. But Caleb is a nice guy. You should give him a chance."

I bite my tongue. If she weren't my sister, I would have so many retorts to that statement.

Like... who said I was looking for a guy to begin with. And... just because he's here and he's kind of cute doesn't mean I'm obligated to give him a chance at anything.

"Are you planning to use all these decorations?" I ask. "Or just pick out some of them?"

"That's Audrey's department. But I vote we pick out a theme and stick with it."

"Good idea."

"Hot chocolate is ready," Audrey says. "Caleb, would you take this over to Brianna?"

Both my sisters are conspiring against me.

Caleb brings over two mugs of hot chocolate. Hands one to me. Then he sits down next to me.

Maybe it's not just my sisters who are conspiring against me.

Maybe it's Caleb, too.

Caleb and my own treacherous heart.

"I haven't see those big old-fashioned bulbs like that

since my grandparents used to put them on their tree. They'll look good on the blue spruce."

I sigh.

"What?" he asks. "What's that about?"

"Nothing. Just nothing. When in Rome…"

"You can't fight it," he says. "Besides, is it really so very bad?"

I look around at my sisters sitting with their boyfriends, all holding mugs of hot chocolate. The scent of the chocolate swirls with the scent of the blue spruce tree and the pleasant scent of the wood smoke from the fireplace.

And I have to swallow a lump in my throat.

The scene is so innocent and serene. Tears sting the back of my eyelids at being part of it. I acknowledge the feelings. What else am I going to do?

But I never ever would have imagined being here in a place like this with my sisters. Not in a million years.

TWENTY-FOUR

Caleb

APPARENTLY AUDREY WORKED out a deal with Claire. In exchange for room and board, Claire will not only do the cleaning she's getting paid for through the trust, but she also will do most of the cooking.

While Claire cooks lasagna, the rest of us work on decorating the tree.

With Bradley on a ladder, Audrey and Bradley string the lights, the big old-fashioned ones that they really had no choice but to use. They're perfect for the big tree.

Wyatt and Lilah work on tying together some of the tree limbs and arranging them along the banisters. Wyatt talked her out of putting tree limbs on the mantle due to the possibility of a fire hazard. Very astute if you ask me.

Audrey has a tendency to keep a blazing fire going and Bradley aids and abets that particular tendency.

Brianna and I are left with the task of sorting decorations.

"It looks like someone went to three different stores and bought one of every possible decoration."

"That's exactly what they did," Brianna says.

"You know this for a fact?" I ask, looking as Brianna as she makes three stacks of decorations. Modern. Farmhouse. And whimsical.

"There's no other explanation," she says, sweeping a hand around the stacks.

"True," I say.

Biscuit stands up from his place in front of the fireplace, shakes, and barks once.

"What's he telling us?" I ask.

"He needs to go outside," Brianna says.

"We can do that," I say. "Want to take a walk in the moonlight?"

"Okay," she says, uncurling her feet from beneath her and standing up.

"We're going to take Biscuit outside for a walk," I say to no one in particular.

"Have fun."

I hold the red coat that I now consider to be Brianna's coat while she slides her arms into it. What was my grandmother's is now hers. It seems fitting somehow. After putting on my own coat, I clip the leash onto the dog's collar.

When she doesn't make any move to button the coat, I hand Brianna the leash and begin buttoning her up.

"Think we'll be outside that long?" she asks.

"You have obviously never accompanied Biscuit on his evening outing."

She smiles and looks into my eyes as I button the buttons on her coat.

There are some things in life that could so easily become one of those habits that a man cherishes and this happens to be one of them.

The simple act of buttoning up Brianna's coat. I can't even remember ever buttoning another girl's coat for her, but with Brianna it just seems like the natural thing to do.

Biscuit barks again, reminding me that I might be lingering a bit too long over those buttons.

I zip up my own coat, then take the leash from Brianna. "I don't trust him not to bolt out of here and pull you down."

"Lilah calls him a horse dog."

"Lilah has a keen sense of observation."

"It's because she sees everything with an artist's eye," Brianna says as we step outside and the sting of the cold wind slams against our skin like a million little needles. The air is colder than I expected it to be. So cold it almost hurts to breath it in.

Brianna takes her gloves out of her pockets and slides them on. I do the same.

"Do you think it's going to snow?" Brianna asks as we follow Biscuit as he makes his way around his route that takes us along the edge of the trees. Not into the trees. Never into the extra darkness of the trees, but away from the light of the motion sensor lights and around the perimeter of the yard.

"I think so," I say. "But not tonight. Tonight it's too cold to snow."

"Too cold to snow. Is that really a thing?"

"Absolutely. The temperature has to be just right."

"Huh." She looks up toward the sky. "Stars," she says. "We don't usually see stars in Houston."

"Now that's a travesty."

"I know." She lowers her gaze back to me, then stops walking.

"What's wrong?" I ask.

"I saw something," she whispers.

"Where?" I keep a firm hold on the dog, reeling him slowly back toward us.

"There," she says. "Near that big maple tree."

"What was it?" I ask.

"I don't know."

Biscuit emits a low growl from deep in his throat, also looking toward the big maple tree.

"An animal or a person?" I ask.

"It's too dark," she says. "I couldn't tell."

"Enough of this," I say. "I'm going over there. Wait here."

I put Biscuit's leash in her hand and take two steps forward toward where she saw something move, toward the large maple tree, my boots crunching on fallen leaves.

"I don't think so," she says, following along after me.

Reaching back, I take her gloved hand. If she's coming with me into the darkness, I won't have her disappearing.

Biscuit moves forward slowly, his ears forward, a low growl in his throat.

TWENTY-FIVE

Brianna

THE GLOW of the moonlight and the bright stars of night light our way as we follow Biscuit along his route in the backyard.

I know the moment the motion sensor light clicks off, leaving us with nothing but the glow of natural light behind us.

I saw something move beneath the trees. I know I did. I just don't know what it was. It was there and then just as quickly, it was gone.

Whatever it was, it sends chills up and down my spine.

The moment I realize Caleb is walking toward the big maple tree where I'd seen the movement, everything inside me protests.

He's not leaving me out here by myself while he walks into the darkness.

Even with the dog to protect me, I'm not letting him leave me out here by myself.

Too many scary movies where the damsel gets left alone after the well-meaning hero gets himself killed by trying to be brave.

As I reach him, he takes my gloved hand firmly in his own gloved hand.

We reach the maple tree, circle it, but find nothing there other than leaves softly fluttering in the breeze.

Caleb pulls out his phone and turns on the flashlight. The light, though, is feeble and doesn't allow us to see anything beyond where we're standing.

"Maybe it was nothing," I say. "Just the wind blowing in the trees."

"Maybe," he says, not moving, straining like I am to see any sign of anything that doesn't belong.

Biscuit is quiet now, just standing here like we are, as though waiting to see what we're going to do.

I shiver.

"They're going to wonder where we are," he says after what seems like a few minutes of standing there, but was probably only a few moments.

"Rightly so."

Just as he goes to turn off the flashlight and put his phone away, I see something shiny reflecting on the ground.

"Wait." I put a hand on his arm.

"What is it?"

"What's that?" I ask. "There. On the ground."

"I don't see anything," he says.

"Shine your light. There. By the tree."

Letting go of his hand, I squat down and study the shiny thing on the ground.

"Don't touch it," he says.

Ignoring him, I reach down and pick it up by the corner.

"What is it?" he asks, holding the light so we can see what's in my hand.

"It's a gum wrapper," I say.

"A gum wrapper? Out here?" He looks out into the trees as though expecting to see whoever dropped the gum wrapper still lurking about.

But there's only the wind brushing through the spruce leaves.

"Are there any more?" he asks, turning back, focusing the light on the ground, moving it around methodically, searching.

"I don't see anything."

He holds out a gloved hand for me to put the gum wrapper in.

"Let's get this inside," he says.

"Okay."

I have a feeling this could be important.

I don't even know anyone who chews gum anymore. Certainly not my sisters. And for a wrapper to be left out here makes no sense. Probably just blown in by the wind.

It could have come from anywhere.

CHAPTER
TWENTY-SIX

Caleb

BRIANNA and I walk straight back to the house, no protest from Biscuit, and don't even stop to take off our coats once we're inside.

I do pause to lock the door behind us.

Brianna unclips Biscuit's leash and he runs straight to his favorite spot in front of the fireplace, turns around three times, and lies down.

As we walk straight and purposeful to the kitchen counter, everyone stops what they're doing to watch us.

"What's up?" Bradley asks.

"Something happened," Wyatt says.

I drop the shiny gum wrapper on the counter and everyone gathers around to look at it.

"Where did you get this?" Audrey asks.

It's rather odd that no one points out how it's strange that we're making a big deal out of a piece of trash we found on the ground. Under normal circumstances... well... nothing is normal here at the moment.

"There's a big maple tree not far into the trees. Due west."

"I know the one," Wyatt says.

We all look at him.

He shrugs. "Biscuit always stops there and sniffs the air."

I look at Wyatt and we all seem to realize the same thing at the same time.

This was not just a piece of trash that the wind randomly blew up to the maple tree. This is something else.

"Can we get prints off of it?" Lilah asks.

"I'm not sure Whiskey Springs has a lab," Brianna says distractedly.

"What about Trent?" Bradley asks Wyatt. "Does he have access to fingerprinting?"

"I can ask him," Wyatt pulls out his phone and walks away to call his friend.

"Why not just give it to the sheriff?" Brianna asks, but I hear the hesitation in her voice. "Never mind. We don't trust him."

"I thought it was just me," Claire says.

"You don't trust him either?" Brianna asks.

"No." Claire shakes her head. "He arrested me. For no reason."

"Right." Brianna narrows her eyes and walks off toward the fireplace.

She stands there a moment, staring into the flames.

"Is she okay?" I ask.

"Thinking," Lilah says.

Wyatt comes back. "Trent knows a guy. We just have to take it into Boulder."

"I can drive it down tomorrow," I say.

"We need to put it in a plastic bag," Audrey says.

Claire goes to the pantry and comes back with one. Hands it to Audrey.

Brianna, still wearing the worn red wool coat, turns around and looks at us, her gaze locking on mine.

"The sheriff chews gum," she says.

"That's right," Claire says. "He does. He's always chewing gum."

"That doesn't necessarily mean anything," Bradley says. "As much as I don't like the guy."

"It doesn't necessarily not mean anything," Wyatt says.

"It means something," I say. "Brianna saw someone..." I glance at her. "Something... near the tree."

"He was out there," Lilah says. "Watching us."

"We can't jump to conclusions," Audrey says.

"The prints won't lie," Brianna says. "If he was out

there, we'll know it. But someone was definitely out there. Biscuit knew it, too."

TWENTY-SEVEN

Brianna

AFTER DINNER, some fine lasagna made by Claire, the six of us sit in front of the fireplace. Claire goes upstairs, taking Blackie with her.

"I told you the sheriff's an ass hat," Wyatt says, tapping the beer bottle in his hand.

"You can't just assume he did it because he's an ass," Audrey says.

"Maybe not, but it definitely makes it seem more likely, doesn't it?" Lilah asks.

"There's definitely something creepy about the guy," I

say, suppressing a little shiver as I remember the way he's stood right here in this room and looked at me.

I don't even want to think about what could have happened if Caleb hadn't shown up when he did.

Probably nothing, but in the moment, I was most definitely creeped out.

"We have to remember that he's dangerous," Audrey says. "He took Biscuit."

There are several murmurs of agreement. The fact that someone kidnapped the dog is certainly something serious enough to keep front and center in our minds.

"And don't forget," Bradley says. "The sheriff arrested Claire AFTER she got out of the hospital."

"Yeah," Audrey agrees. "That never made any sense."

"You're certain she didn't have anything to do with the notes?" I ask.

"She didn't do it," Audrey says. "She couldn't have. She was in the hospital."

"Why did he arrest her?" I ask, staring into the flames.

I'm sitting close enough that my shoulder rests against Caleb's.

Bradley and Wyatt are drinking a beer, but the rest of us are just drinking water.

"I have an idea about that," Bradley says. "I think he wanted to make us think she did it. To plant the possibility that she did it. To distract us."

"That makes a lot of sense," I say. "Except did he not think we'd figure out she couldn't have done it?"

"He was probably just hoping," Lilah says, covering her mouth to hide a yawn.

"I don't trust him," Wyatt says. "That's just the be all and end all of it."

"Do you think he saw us?" I ask Caleb, circling back around to the maple tree where we'd found the gum wrapper.

"I have no reason to think he didn't."

"Then that means he knows we know," I say.

"Maybe. It was dark. It depends on whether he hid or if he ran. If he ran, he might not have seen us looking. Might not have seen us find the gum wrapper."

"But if he stayed and hid. To watch us..." I say, letting the idea linger.

"Then he might know we know something. But he won't know for sure that we put it all together."

"Unless he bugged the house again," Wyatt says.

We all look at him.

"Claire's house fire. We were all over there while he was here."

"That's right," I say. "He was here. Sitting outside. Doesn't mean he hadn't been inside the house."

"He probably has cameras along the road and knew we were on our way to the house," Caleb says.

"We can't do anything about it tonight," Wyatt says, kissing Lilah on the top of the head. "I need to get this one up to bed."

"We all need to get some rest," Audrey says.

"Do you have a long drive?" I ask, looking into Caleb's stormy blue eyes.

"Not so long," he says. "Just down the mountain."

I cringe, remembering the steep drop off on the side of the road. I pull out my phone to see what the weather says. It was clear earlier, but that doesn't mean it's still clear.

"Caleb," Audrey says. "There's no need for you to drive this late. Sleep here on the sofa."

"We need to set up that guest room like we talked about," Bradley says.

"Where would we set up a guest room?" Lilah asks.

"We're thinking about building a maid's quarters behind the kitchen. Claire could live there. We haven't talked to her about it yet. We're just thinking about it."

"It's a good idea," I say. "You need to keep a guest room available."

Wyatt stands up, pulling Lilah up with him. To my surprise, he picks her up, bridal style, and carries her off up the stairs. "Good night," he says over his shoulder.

"Well," I say.

"You don't have to carry me," Audrey says with amusement.

"Don't worry, Love. I was planning on making you walk."

"Good night," Audrey says after rolling her eyes at Bradley. "There are blankets and a pillow tucked in that ottoman."

"I'll think about it," Caleb says. "Thank you."

"She's right, you know," I say as my sister and her fiancé walk upstairs. "It's safer if you stay here."

"You just trying to get me to spend the night?"

"No," I say. "I'm just thinking about those steep roads. But you can go if you want to."

"I'm thinking maybe I'll just sleep here."

"Okay," I say with a shrug as though it doesn't matter to me one way or the other.

And, of course, it doesn't matter.

"I have to be careful, though," he says.

"Why is that?"

"That's what happened to my brothers."

"What happened?"

"Sleeping over one night for one reason or another. Then... here they are."

"I think they had other reasons for staying over than a late night with possible fog on the road."

"They stayed to make sure the girls were safe. You're right."

"You'd be staying to make sure *you're* safe."

He narrows his eyes at me. "And just what makes you so sure about that?"

I feel a bit of heat rise to my cheeks as I look into his eyes. "It's what we said." I make an effort to swallow the lump in my throat.

"We say a lot of things."

A log falls, sending embers scattering up the chimney.

"They left their dog down here," I say. "Either they forgot him or they're planning on you staying."

"I don't think they forgot him."

"No." I shake my head. "They wouldn't forget him."

"I guess that settles it then," he says.

"How so?"

"I guess I'm staying. Can't leave the dog down here by himself."

I smirk at him, then drop onto the floor to slide open the ottoman. Just as Audrey said, there's a blanket, two actually, and a pillow tucked inside.

I stack them on the sofa behind me. "Do you need anything else?" I ask.

Biscuit snores softly in his sleep and turns over.

When Caleb doesn't answer, I turn around to face him.

He's focused on me with those stormy blue eyes.

I lift an eyebrow.

His gaze dips ever so briefly down to my lips and a bevy of drunken butterflies scatter in my stomach.

"Stay with me for a bit," he says.

Since I can't think of anything I'd like more, I sit down next to him, pulling my stockinged feet up under me.

He unfolds one of the blankets and wraps it over us.

When he puts his arm around me, I rest my head against his shoulder.

There are things a girl can fight and things maybe a girl should fight.

Then there are things that just quite simply should be allowed to run their course.

TWENTY-EIGHT

Caleb

"Want to watch a movie?" I ask after Brianna rests her cheek on my shoulder.

"Okay," she says, but doesn't move.

I hear people walking around upstairs. My brothers and her sisters are upstairs getting ready for bed, leaving us alone down here with their dog.

The shades are all down, which is rather a shame, considering that they're blocking what could be a wonderful view of the mountains in the moonlight.

The reasons for the shades are sound. Anyone, perhaps

even the sheriff, could be standing outside watching us through the windows.

"I left my window shade up last night," Brianna murmurs against my shoulder.

"You're quite the rebel aren't you?"

She smells good. Like lavender with a hint of spruce from being outside today and messing around with the tree limbs.

The tree in the corner looks good there. So far it only has lights on. Big oversized lights that harken from another era. Blue. Green. Red. Yellow. They don't even blink, but they don't need to.

Tomorrow it'll have decorations on it. I don't which theme they'll go with, but it won't matter. Whatever they go with, the tree will still look old-fashioned. In a good way. With those oversized lights, it has no other choice than to look old-fashioned. Like bringing the past and present together.

Like the well-worn red wool coat that Brianna wears. The one that belonged to my grandmother.

I like it that she wears it. Not only does it suit her, but I like the idea that Brianna is wearing something that belonged to someone I loved.

It feels like a natural continuity.

When I kiss her on the top of her head, she sighs.

"I told myself I wasn't going to do this," she murmurs.

"Do what? Sit in front of the fireplace on a cold winter

evening? With an oversized blue spruce Christmas tree taking up half the living room?"

She smiles, but doesn't lift her gaze. "Something like that."

"If it's any consolation, I told myself the same thing."

"Did you now?" She tilts her head up to look into my eyes.

"I did. I refused to risk following my brothers' footsteps."

"And yet here you are."

"Yes," I say with a little smile. "Here I am."

"And here I am."

"In my defense," I say. "No one warned me."

"No one warned you that spending time with your family could be hazardous?"

"Are you a hazard now?"

"I've been called worse." She lowers her head, snuggling her cheek against my shoulder.

"I'm going to have to kick someone's ass yet. I can see it coming."

She puts a hand on my arm and closes her eyes.

"Warned you about what?" she asks.

"Oh. Let's see. That the Sinclair women have some kind of spell they weave around the Winslow men. Or that the mysterious sister is a beautiful goddess in disguise as a mere mortal to most men."

"You have a very active imagination," she says.

"You have no idea."
I already know that I'm lost to her.
Kissing her would be a very bad idea.
Kissing her would only make things worse.
A very bad idea.

TWENTY-NINE

Brianna

Maybe I should have known all along what I was missing.

Maybe if I hadn't had my head stuck in the proverbial sand of city life, I would have realized that there was a good reason both of my sisters came up here to Whiskey Springs and stayed. They just stayed.

For a lot of reasons, obviously. But taking away the inheritance and its stipend, it's easy to see why they wanted to stay.

Even with the danger of someone threatening them, trying to get them to leave, it's easy to see why.

Maybe it's the Winslow men.

Or maybe that's just a part of it.

It's definitely part of it.

Sitting here in front of the warm fire would be cozy in and of itself, but sitting here in front of the warm fire wouldn't be nearly so alluring if I wasn't in the arms of the handsome Caleb Winslow.

I'm doing exactly what I said I wasn't going to do.

I'm falling for the brother of my sisters' boyfriends.

I'm not even sure what I'm going to do with my life now that I've been fired from my job and moved away from Houston, leaving everything I knew.

But this place has a charm I hadn't expected. Sure. I saw the videos my sisters sent. I spent time on the phone with them. Hearing the roar of the river and the chirping of the birds in the background.

But there are things I had no way of understanding without actually being here.

The way the cold mountain air is so clean it almost burns the lungs. The scent of the blue spruce trees that smell better than any of the candles we burned at Christmastime.

The way the fire crackles in the fireplace, sending little fireworks of embers up through the chimney.

I understand now why they won't let anyone run them off.

Between the inheritance and the Winslow men and the cozy fireplace. The danger just seems to pale in comparison.

Not that something doesn't need to be done about the

danger. It does. And finding that gum wrapper just put it all together for me. I know I just got here and I don't expect to be the one to just swoop in and solve everything, but I think I'm onto something.

The question, of course, is why. Why would the sheriff care who lives here? Why would he go to all the trouble of buying bird drones and dropping off threatening notes? Why would he kidnap the dog just to frighten everyone?

It makes no sense.

There has to be something we're missing.

"I can feel you thinking," Caleb says.

"You do not."

"Convince me you're not thinking too much right now."

I lift my head from his shoulder and look into his stormy blue eyes. Eyes that seem to be so calm right now.

"I..." I forget what I was going to say as he lowers his face to mine and his breath mingles with mine.

Knowing he's going to kiss me makes my whole system overheat and come undone.

Everything else disappears into the background, leaving only us.

The sound of my sisters and their boyfriends walking around upstairs as they get ready for bed. The fire crackling the fireplace. Biscuit whimpering softly as he has puppy dreams.

The whole world comes down to just Caleb and me. Nothing else matters. Nothing else exists.

He gently puts a hand on my cheek and my eyes flutter closed.

When his lips touch mine, it feels like everything fits together, everything in my life up to this point fits together like the scattered pieces of a puzzle that suddenly make sense.

With a little sigh, I yield to the feel of his lips against mine.

So right.

Nothing has ever felt so right.

THIRTY

Caleb

KISSING BRIANNA IS my new favorite bad idea.

What I'd tried to convince myself was a bad idea is now the best idea I think I've ever had.

Her lips are so soft and sweet beneath mine. So yielding.

Now that I've kissed her, I don't think I ever want to stop. I don't think I could stop if I wanted to.

But, truly, why would I want to?

I shift her a bit so that her legs are across mine and I have better access to that mouth of hers.

So smart. She's one of the smartest people I've ever met. And the most beautiful.

And now kissing her is like the best thing I've ever done.

I don't know how much time passes. When I do notice things around us, I know that the house is quiet. That the fire has burned down to a normal glow.

"There's a problem," I say, replacing my lips with my fingertip.

"No problem," she says, making me smile.

"I don't ever want to stop kissing you."

"Good problem," she says, turning so that she kisses the palm of my hand. "to have."

"Agreed," I murmur, putting my lips back on hers.

I lean her back on the couch, exploring her wonderful, delicious mouth. My tongue caressing hers. Touching the roof of her mouth, making her gasp a little.

When the clock chimes Midnight, I know we have to stop.

At least for now.

"I should walk you to your room," I say.

"Okay," she murmurs against my lips.

"You're not making this easy."

"No," she says.

"Is it possible to get drunk on kissing?" I ask.

"Yes."

"Alright." I give her little kisses on the edge of her lips. On her cheeks. On her eyelids. "You're going to hate me tomorrow if I don't let you get some sleep."

"Sleep is overrated."

"So says the woman drunk on kissing."

I manage to disentangle us and get us both to our feet.

"Shall I carry you up the stairs to your room?"

She looks over her shoulder toward the stairs. "That will take some practice. I don't think you're ready."

"Okay." I take her hand firmly in mine. "Another time then."

"Yes. Another time."

We walk through the shadowed room to the stairs, then start up.

"Has anyone ever told you you're a bad influence?" I ask.

"If you say that, you might have to kick your own ass."

"You might be right." We reach the top of the stairs. "You going to ride into Boulder with me tomorrow?" I ask, knowing I don't have to explain why.

"Wild horses," she says.

"Does that mean yes?"

"Yes, but…" We stop in front of her room. "I think I need a goodnight kiss first."

"I think you've had enough kissing for one night," I tell her.

She pouts prettily and opens her door.

I pull her back against me. "Don't say I didn't warn you."

The clock is striking one o'clock before I find the fortitude and discipline or whatever it is that's required to finally tell her goodnight.

My head is so full of Brianna as I leave her room and

make my way back downstairs, that I don't hear the back door open.

THIRTY-ONE

Brianna

"It's gone."

"What's gone?" I ask, sleepily, heading for the coffee machine.

"The gum wrapper," Audrey says.

"What do you mean it's gone? Did someone throw it out?" I obviously did not get enough sleep last night to be dealing with whatever crisis Audrey has going on this morning.

Audrey leans her hands on the kitchen island and looks right at me. "Brianna. The gum wrapper is gone."

Something in her voice has me turning around and facing her.

"Where did you hide it?" I have no doubt that Audrey hid it somewhere.

She opens the cabinet where she keeps the coffee mugs. "Here," she says. "Behind the mugs."

"No one took it," I say, pulling the coffee mugs out of the cabinet, one by one, looking inside each one. Determined to prove that it's just misplaced. "Is anyone else up?"

"No. We're the first ones."

"Huh." Not surprising for me. I get up early every morning to get ready to go to work. It's not a habit that I'm going to break anytime soon. But Audrey. "Why are you up?"

"Sometimes I just wake up."

"Is Bradley up?"

"He's in the shower. He hasn't been down yet."

I look over toward the sectional. "When did Caleb leave?"

"He was gone when I got up. I don't know."

I nod. Thinking. Putting the coffee mugs back on the shelf and going to the next shelf above it.

"It's not here," Audrey says.

"Is Claire up yet?" I whisper.

"I haven't seen anyone else." Audrey pushes her hair back off her face. "You were the last one to leave down here last night. You and Caleb."

"You hid it. So no one else knew where it was. Caleb is

supposed to take it in to Boulder today, but I'm supposed to go with him."

"Maybe he got up, made coffee, found it, and left with it."

I run a hand over my still swollen lips. "He wouldn't do that."

Audrey studies me a moment. Then turns her eyes toward the ceiling with a sigh. Not quite an eye roll. Almost.

"Who else?" Audrey asks.

"Claire," I say. "As much as I don't like the sheriff, maybe he knows something we don't."

Audrey shakes her head. "Claire wouldn't do it."

"Did she see where you hid it?" I choose a mug and start making my coffee.

"I'm sure she did. She sort of just blends into the background."

Audrey and I stop talking as someone starts down the stairs.

"Good morning," Claire says, coming into the kitchen. "Can I make breakfast?"

"That would be nice," Audrey says. "If you feel up to it."

"I don't mind a bit." She goes to the refrigerator and starts pulling out eggs and bacon and butter.

Audrey and I look at each other.

"Claire," Audrey says. "We can't find the gum wrapper."

"What?" Claire asks, setting the eggs carefully on the counter. "You put up there. Behind the coffee mugs."

"It's not there."

"Let me see." She starts pulling the mugs out of the cabinet just as I had.

Audrey and I stand back and let her look. I finish making my coffee and take a sip.

"Have you had coffee?" I ask Audrey.

"No."

I shove my mug into her hands. "Take this one." I grab another mug and make another cup for myself.

"I don't understand," Claire says. "Maybe Mr. Caleb took it in to Boulder already."

"He didn't," I say. "I'm supposed to go with him."

"Oh." Claire looks at me. Then Audrey. "You think I did it."

"No," Audrey says, putting a hand on her arm. "I don't think you took it."

"You have every right to think so. I'll pack my things and get out of here." She turns around, her gaze landing on the carton of eggs. "But I'll make breakfast first."

"No," Audrey says. "Claire. We don't think you took it. We just need you to help us figure out what happened to it."

"I haven't seen any rats around here," she says.

I hide a smile behind my coffee mug. This is going to be interesting.

I walk to the window overlooking the backyard. The shades are already up—apparently they're on some kind of timer. And the view out over the meadow past the trees, looking over toward the forever snow-capped peaks, is nothing short of spectacular. With the way the early morning sunshine glitters on the dewy ground, everything just sparkles.

Audrey was gifted one of the most beautiful places I've ever seen.

No one is going to run her away from here. No one.

And I just might include myself in that. No one is going to run me away from here either.

I've hardly even seen the little town of Whiskey Springs, other than the drive up here, but I don't need to.

This is one of those places a person could call home.

THIRTY-TWO

Caleb

SINCE I HADN'T BROUGHT any extra clothes with me yesterday, and I woke up early, I just dashed home for a shower and a change of clothes.

I can be back before anyone even realizes I'm gone.

While I'm there, I toss a couple of changes of clothes in a duffle bag and throw it into the backseat of my truck.

Presumptuous? Maybe. I prefer to think of myself as prepared. Knowing I've got to drive into Boulder today to take the gum wrapper, I don't know what time I'll be back. Especially so since I'm going to be taking Brianna.

The thought makes me smile to myself.

I don't even care that I was wrong.

I had been wrong for thinking that I would absolutely positively not be interested in the third Sinclair sister.

Talk about saving the best for last.

They saved the best for last.

Brianna is beautiful and kind and smarter than anybody I know.

Not to mention the way she kisses.

She looks like a goddess and kisses like a siren.

Maybe I have my metaphors mixed up, but I don't care.

I drive over the narrows, secretly hoping I'm on the side of the Sinclair house when the roads close. And they will. One good snowfall and this road won't be passable.

I can still get there, though. I can put on some snow-shoes and hike in and out.

After parking in front of the house, I knock on the door.

Claire answers the door.

I was not prepared for the activity level going on inside the house.

So much for slipping back inside unnoticed.

"I'm so glad you're back," Claire says.

"Why? What's going on?"

"They'll tell you," she says and leaves me standing there. "I've got bacon cooking."

Bradley, Audrey sitting next to him, is sitting on the sectional, his eyes glued to the iPad. A closer look tells me he's looking at the security cameras.

My stomach twists.

"What happened?" I ask.

Wyatt and Lilah are at the dining table having breakfast.

But I don't see Brianna.

Bradley doesn't answer. I don't think he heard me.

I walk to the dining table and ask Wyatt.

"What happened?" I ask again.

"The gum wrapper is missing."

"Missing? How does a gum wrapper go missing? Where's Brianna?"

"Upstairs getting dressed," Lilah says.

Relief floods through me.

I guess I'd been worried that something had happened to her.

"Sit down," Claire says. "Have some breakfast."

I sit down. "I'll wait for Brianna," I say.

"Brianna already ate," Claire says as she puts a plate with eggs and bacon in front of me. "Eat up."

As I scoop up a forkful of scrambled eggs, it occurs to me that Wyatt and Lilah wouldn't be calmly having breakfast if something had happened to Brianna.

Maybe it's my brain that's gotten scrambled.

"How did the gum wrapper go missing?" I ask. "Did someone throw it away?"

Lilah looks at me and shrugs.

If I ever wanted a role model for being unconcerned about things, it would have to be Lilah. I don't know what she's feeling on the inside, but on the outside, she presents as calm, cool, and collected.

Then I hear Brianna coming down the stairs and my attention is focused completely on her.

Just seeing her coming down the stairs makes the whole room light up.

CHAPTER

THIRTY-THREE

Brianna

Showered, hair blow dried, and maybe straightened a little more than necessary—I tell myself it's a habit honed from years of getting ready for work. Nothing to do with my planned trip into Boulder today with Caleb and certainly nothing to do with simply seeing Caleb.

Without the gum wrapper, there is no longer a reason for driving into Boulder.

Instead, everyone is doing what they can to figure out what happened.

Bradley is going over the security camera footage, looking for any sign of anyone coming in the house.

My question is how in the world would whoever came into the house know where to look for the gum wrapper.

Wyatt has already called his friend Trent and Trent is trying to get away to come up here to see what he can see.

No one has called the police.

Hello. We'd like to report a crime. We found an empty gum wrapper outside and now it's missing.

Ah. No. We are truly on our own on this one. And now I'm seeing more clearly why Audrey and Bradley are trying to solve this by themselves.

Especially with the town's sheriff being their primary suspect now, they certainly can't report it. Not to him.

I reach the top of the stairs and do one of those automatic scans of the room.

My gaze stops when I see Caleb, looking right at me, sitting at the dining table.

He smiles and my heart does summersaults.

After hours of kissing last night, he's been pretty much all I've thought about.

I'm disappointed, a little, that he and I won't be going into Boulder. But. He's here. And as long as he's here, I don't mind staying home.

And I don't mind that I'm thinking about my sister's house as home.

I even unpacked some of my clothes already, hanging them in the closet. That seemed to do it. Home is where your clothes are hanging.

I reach the dining room table and sit down next to Caleb.

"I guess they told you," I say.

"Someone stole the gum wrapper."

"Yes. I guess that means someone got into the house again."

"That's why they take the pets upstairs with them at night and lock the doors."

"You were down here," I say. "By yourself. You didn't hear anything."

"I heard nothing. Either I was sleeping or upstairs."

"I don't understand why the cameras didn't catch him."

"He probably put another scrambler on the house," Wyatt says. "Trent can tell us that."

"So whoever took the gum wrapper is most likely the guilty party," I say.

"If anyone heard us talking about gum wrappers like this, they'd think we'd lost our minds," Caleb says.

"What people think is irrelevant," I say, looking at Lilah.

She gives me a little nod of agreement.

"I guess we won't be going into Boulder," I say.

"I've already been recruited to help decorate the tree."

"Really? Is that something you have experience in?" I ask.

"Not even a little. I'm counting on having someone teach me the ropes."

"I decorated a tree once," I say, picking up a slice of bacon off his plate and biting into it.

"The blind leading the blind," he says. "Always a good sign."

"Might as well have fun with it," I say, going over to the coffee machine to make myself a second cup of coffee.

CHAPTER
THIRTY-FOUR

Caleb

AFTER BREAKFAST, I head outside with Wyatt to chop some firewood.

"One thing about being with the Sinclair girls," Wyatt says, balancing a piece of wood on a stump. "It takes a lot of firewood."

"I noticed," I say. I'm also noticing that my brother is tutoring me on the Sinclair girls. Seems to me like he's making some assumptions. I tell him so.

"You're assuming I need to know these things."

Wyatt brings the axe down, deftly dropping two pieces of wood on either side of the stump.

"The signs are all there, Bro."

"I don't know about signs."

Wyatt picks up the two logs and puts them back on the stump to make another chop for kindling.

"You're a lot more like Bradley than you are me."

"I can't tell if that's an insult."

He brings the axe down. "Just an observation. He resisted admitting how he feels about Audrey."

"I just met Brianna two days ago," I say.

"Spontaneous combustion." He hauls the axe back and lets it down easy, making little splices for kindling.

"And if I admit I like her?"

"You don't have to tell me. I already know it." He gathers up the little pieces of kindling and puts them in a stack out of the way.

I adjust my coat. Gaze out toward the trees around the perimeter of the yard, then up toward the snow-capped mountain peaks that almost look like they're close enough to reach out and touch. Maybe just a short little hike. Of course, it's so very much further and treacherous.

I shake my head. Looks are deceiving.

What is it about his whole gum wrapper thing that we're missing?

Maybe we aren't missing anything. Maybe whoever is doing it is just covering his tracks. He knows we found the gum wrapper and he retrieved it. Evidence. He retrieved the evidence.

"You really think the sheriff has something to do with all this?"

"If I was a betting man, I'd put money on it."

"What makes you so sure?" I ask.

"It all adds up," he says, dropping the axe through the middle of a piece of wood, letting it crash to the sides onto the ground.

"Okay." I tilt my collar up to cover my ears. "Let's say you figure out that it is him. What are you going to do about it? He's the law around here."

"I guess we'll have to take it to the county authorities."

"The sheriff is closer to Bradley's age. What? A couple of years older? What does he think?"

"He definitely thinks it's the sheriff."

"You could confront him," I say.

"That won't help. We need evidence."

"The cameras. But he keeps sabotaging the cameras."

Wyatt adds more kindling for his stack.

"I think you're just avoiding talking about your crush on Brianna."

"Is that why you wanted me to come out here with you? To talk about my crush on Brianna?"

"No," he says. "I need you to hand me that log behind you."

I hand him the log.

"You want to take a swing?" he asks. "See if you can still split a log?

"Nah. I'm good."

"It'll make you feel better."

"I feel fine."

He slams the axe down again. "I was thinking."

"Never a good sign."

"This house is plenty big for all of us. You could work from here."

"Not enough room for all of us to work from here."

"Sure it is. Lilah and I are building the greenhouse and flower shop. You could build an separate office if you need your own space."

"Does Audrey know you're building a whole community up here?"

"It was her idea."

I scowl at my brother. "Which part?"

"All of it. She asked me to talk to you."

THIRTY-FIVE

Brianna

"What are you doing?" Lilah asks as I type on my phone.

I feel like I could ask her the same thing. Lilah has a box of live flowers that cost God knows how much money to have shipped here, arranging them in a vase, using a YouTube video as a guide.

"Filling out an application." My gaze flicks past her to where Wyatt is chopping firewood and Caleb is standing nearby. "What are they talking about?"

"I don't know," Lilah says with a little shrug. "Guy talk. What kind of application?"

"I'm trying to find a job."

"In Whiskey Springs?"

"Yes." I go back to filling in my experience which is vast.

"Brianna," Lilah says, leaning toward me. "Where's your car?"

"My car?" My fingers hesitate on the screen.

"Yes. Your car. Where's your car?"

"I left it at a used car lot. They're trying to sell it for me."

Lilah puts her palm against her forehead. "Are you serious?"

"Yes. I did some work for the owner and he was willing to help me out."

"So how do you plan to get to work?"

"I'll take your car," I say, mostly just to annoy her.

"My car isn't winterized." I look at her blankly and she explains. "It needs new windshield wipers. Winter tires. An emergency kit."

"What's an emergency kit?"

"Blankets. Candles. Food and water."

"It's not that far into town," I say, feeling a bit queasy at her implication that blankets and food and water are required to get a car ready to just drive into town.

"Maybe. But it's far enough that you could be less than a mile away and snowed in for days."

"I have a cell phone. I'd call you."

Lilah huffs out a breath. "We wouldn't be able to get to you. I'm trying to make a point."

"And your point is?"

"My point is you shouldn't be applying for jobs. You should work here."

"Doing what?" I ask, sitting back in my chair.

"I don't know, but you have enough experience doing a million different things, surely there's something you could do from home."

"I don't know what it would be. So. I thought you were coming up here to draw and paint."

"I am drawing and painting. But this is fun, too."

I narrow my eyes at her. "You just like having something to do with Wyatt."

"Is that so wrong? To have a project to do with someone you love?" She pulls the flowers out of the vase and starts the video over.

There. She said it.

"So Bradley and Audrey are engaged. Are you and Wyatt...?"

She smiles broadly, but keeps her voice low. "Yes. But we're giving Audrey a minute in the spotlight before we announce it."

"Audrey's not blind," I say.

Lilah pauses her video. "Maybe we'll have a double wedding. Or a triple wedding."

"What? Is Claire getting married, too?" I know she's not talking about Claire, but I can't resist being purposely obtuse.

"Not Claire." Lilah rolls her eyes and starts her video back up. "You."

"Something's wrong with you."

"Maybe it's not me that something's wrong with."

"It would be too weird. Three brothers and three sisters. It's not natural."

"Okay. So you'd rather swipe left and swipe right hoping to find someone you like who happens to live close enough to have a relationship with than just pick the one who's standing in front of you. Just because he happens to be the brother of you sisters' husbands?"

I don't answer her.

I don't answer because I don't have anything to say in defense of that.

THIRTY-SIX

Caleb

"I THOUGHT you said you didn't have any experience in tree decorating."

I'm standing on a ladder while Brianna hands me little bird decorations to attach to the upper tree limbs.

"I think I might have said I have limited experience. There might be a difference."

"Maybe it's a case of birds of a feather flock together." I'm referring to the way I'd grouped the birds close together.

"Maybe," she says. "Come down."

"What? You're firing me already?"

"No. I'm going to demonstrate by doing."

"A lady shouldn't climb ladders," I say as I climb down.

"It's okay. It's the twenty-first century."

"You're putting a lot of trust in this old wooden ladder," I say as she starts up and the ladder wobbles.

"I'm actually putting my trust in you."

Her trust is not misplaced. I'd throw myself beneath the ladder before I'd let her fall to the ground.

She moves one of the birds two inches to the right.

"There," she says. "Does that look better from down there?"

"I can't tell any difference. I think you moved that bird over two inches though."

She gives me a vexed look that only makes me smile.

I've ever known anyone who looks so beautiful when she's vexed.

She moves one of the other birds over a little bit, too. "Would you hand me another one?"

"Another bird? Yes. And maybe one of those little pinecones."

I hand her the bird first. Then the pinecone.

"Somebody is here," I say. Someone driving a truck pulls up to the front of the house.

"Probably Trent."

"Probably. This should be interesting."

"I think the sheriff put up another scrambler while everyone was over at Claire's house," she says, taking one step down.

"Do you think he burned Claire's house on purpose?"

"Yes. Want to help me down? I want to hear what he has to say."

I turn back to her just in time to see the ladder wobble and tilt back.

In one single instant, I realize that she's going to fall. And I only have a second, tops, to prevent it.

Putting out my arms, one hand under her knees, one under her shoulders, I catch her and swing her out of the way of the ladder just before it clatters to the ground.

Her arms around me, she looks at me with her teal blue eyes.

"You saved me," she says with an amused expression.

If I didn't know better, I would think she orchestrated this just so she could end up in my arms.

"Everything okay?" Lilah rushes over in time to see the ladder lying on the floor.

She looks from the ladder to us. Raises an eyebrow and continues her way toward the door.

Brianna looks at me and shrugs.

"What was that about?" I ask her.

"I have no idea."

With her being this close, I have no choice but to kiss her.

She closes her eyes as I lower my lips to hers, giving her a chaste kiss, suitable for public display.

"Wyatt thinks I should move in," I say.

"So does Lilah."

"He said it was Audrey's idea."

"You know how it is with people in relationships. They're always trying to fix people up."

"I've noticed that." I lower her gently to her feet as Trent comes inside the house.

He takes one look at the ladder on the floor.

"Everything okay?" he asks.

"We're going to need a new ladder," I say.

THIRTY-SEVEN

Brianna

WHILE TRENT SWEEPS the house for bugs, I help Audrey and Lilah make sandwiches. Claire had to drive into town to take care of some paperwork regarding her house fire.

"Do you really think Claire's okay?" I ask, slicing a tomato.

"I think so," Audrey says. "She's really tough. And I think she rather likes living here."

"Maybe she didn't feel safe living by herself."

"I can see why," Audrey says, taking a stack of plates out of the cabinet. "She was arrested for something she couldn't have done."

"I don't think she has it in her to be threatening," Lilah says. "She's a very kind person."

"Are you really going to build her a maid's quarters?" I ask, keeping any thoughts to the contrary about Claire to myself.

"I'm thinking yes. If not for her, then for somebody."

"You like having somebody to cook and clean," I say.

"Don't you?" Audrey asks.

"Don't be defensive. I'm just asking. We never had anyone to help out when we were growing up. So. It's different. I'm just asking."

"I know," Audrey says with a sigh. "I shouldn't feel guilty about it. But yes. I do like someone to keep the house clean and to do the heavy cooking."

"Nothing wrong with that," Lilah says. "I always thought I'd have a big house and a housekeeper when I grew up. I sort of thought everybody did."

We both look blankly at her.

"I can't help what I thought. I just assumed that I'd have it someday."

"Even though we didn't," I say.

"You're questioning the logic of a child."

"Well," Audrey says. "I guess as long as you stay here, you'll have that. It's in the trust."

"That remind me," I say. "I don't remember reading in the paperwork about what happens to the house if you decided you didn't want to live here anymore."

"I don't remember seeing that either," Lilah says, putting pickles on a plate. "It should have been there though." She looks at me. "You spent the most time going through it. There wasn't anything?"

"No." I open a loaf of bread and pull out a half a dozen slices. Then I do a quick count in my head and pull out six more.

"That won't be enough," Audrey says. "Guys eat more than we do."

"I know," I say. "It's just weird how much food it takes to feed everyone."

"I don't mind though," Lilah says. "I thought it might be weird, but it's not. It's kind of nice having everyone here."

"I agree," Audrey says. "I thought I wanted some time to myself. but I'm glad we're all here together now."

"I'm glad, too," I say. "I think it would be a good idea to call your attorney and find out the answer to what happens in the event someone did convince you to leave. You have his number, right? Andrew Harrington."

"Of course I have his number." She looks toward the stairs where the men are going through the house.

"Last time he was here, he wore a disguise," Audrey says. "Not this time. If the house if bugged, he'll know we know."

"There are more of us here now," Lilah says.

"We already know he's bold," Audrey says.

"I don't think anyone is *that* bold," Lilah says.

"I think I'm going to take a walk down to the river while they finish up," I say. "I'll take Biscuit."

I just need to clear my head. To have a few minutes alone with my own thoughts.

"Sure," Audrey says. "I'll call you if they get finished before you come back."

"Thanks, Audrey," I say.

All I have to do is grab Biscuit's leash and he's up racing toward the back door, ready to go outside.

The horse dog, as Lilah calls him, is ready to go outside. Lilah has warmed up to Biscuit, but she still seems to prefer the company of the cat over the dog. Not surprising. We never had a dog growing up. A cat, but not a dog.

I step outside into the cool air and warm sunshine, an odd juxtaposition that still surprises me.

I follow the dog who knows the way and seems to know that we're heading to the river.

Reaching the river bank, the rushing water blocks out all other sounds behind me.

I sit down on a sun-warmed boulder and watch the water swirl around the rocks. Biscuit sits down next to me.

When an elk walks up to the bank across from us, I put an arm around the dog to keep him from reacting, but Biscuit doesn't seem to either notice or care about the elk.

I like it here. A lot. That surprises me.

I also like Caleb Winslow. That surprises me even more.

And it surprises me that I don't want to change that. It's

not that I want to have what my sisters have. I'm my own person.

I just like Caleb. I'd like him in Houston and I like him here.

He's kind and sweet and makes me smile.

Maybe I'm at a different place in my life than I've ever been before. Not so focused on work. That could have something to do with it. Whatever it is, I'm okay with it.

As for work, I don't know what I'm going to do.

I guess I don't have to figure anything out right now. I have some savings. And Audrey has the house. As long as I'm here, I don't have to worry about paying rent. So my savings will last that much longer. Until I figure out what I'm going to do.

Trent should be finished sweeping the house by now and I really want to hear what he has to say.

Standing up, I stretch and turn around. Biscuit stands up, too, and shakes.

We have to walk through a grove of spruce trees to get back to the house. It's cooler in the shade and I put my hands in the pockets of my red wool coat.

Someone steps out from behind one of the trees, blocking my way.

"What are you doing here?" I ask. Biscuit barks twice. "We were just talking about you."

Andrew Harrington, wearing jeans and a heavy coat, stands in front of me. I almost don't even recognize him.

Then Biscuit's leash slips out of my hand as someone grabs me from behind.

"Run, Biscuit," I say, but someone has me by the throat and the words come out as a whisper.

"Get out of here, you mutt," the man holding me says.

My blood chills. I recognize that voice.

THIRTY-EIGHT

Caleb

I FOLLOW BRADLEY, Wyatt, and Trent back downstairs.

Trent is holding a scrambler he pulled out of the attic. Apparently whoever left the first scrambler there replaced the old one that Trent had disabled. Must have thought the old one had gone bad.

"I'm just glad you didn't find any more cameras," Bradley says.

"I guess he decided it wasn't a good route to go," Wyatt says. "Since we obviously caught onto that particular scheme."

"Right," Trent says. "Anybody can buy little bug detectors now."

"Where's Biscuit?" Bradley asks, reaching the first floor.

"Brianna took him for a walk," Lilah says. "I'll call her."

"By herself?" I ask, my heart slamming into my throat. I thought we'd decided that no one would go anywhere alone.

"She just wanted a minute to herself," Audrey says.

Lilah bites her bottom lip. "It has been a little while. She should be back by now."

I'm already putting on my coat. As I throw open the back door, I see Biscuit racing toward me, his leash dragging behind him.

"Something's happened to Brianna," I shout just before I take off running toward the direction the dog had come from.

I vaguely hear footsteps behind me, a little delayed.

Instinctively, I run toward the river, hitting the trail running through the trees, directly toward the river.

What I see as I round a curve in the trail, chills me to the bone. My breath coming in gasps, I stop and take a step back to give me time to assess the situation.

I see Brianna, wearing her faded red wool coat, in a choke hold.

The sheriff. The sheriff has her in a choke hold. There's another man in front of her, a man I don't recognize.

"I told you I don't want this to be violent," the unrecognized man says.

"Sometimes violence is necessary," Sheriff Morgan says.

"No. I won't go to prison because you were stupid."

"I'm the sheriff. I say who goes to prison."

Bradley and Wyatt come up behind me. I hold up a hand behind me to stop them.

They stand quietly, also taking in the situation.

I hear the women coming up behind them. We're all here now.

It's time for me to put a stop to whatever is going on.

"I'm going in," I say to whoever is listening.

"You don't have a weapon," Bradley says.

"Doesn't need one," Wyatt says. "He's got us."

As I step forward, they fall in at my sides like shadows.

"Let her go," I demand, my words cutting through the charged air.

"We're just having a conversation," the unidentified man says.

"Doesn't look like much of a conversation," I say easily. "Seeing as how Brianna can't get a word out."

"We're just sending a message," the unidentified man says.

"Message sent and received," I say. "Now let her go."

Sheriff Morgan shifts, but doesn't let go.

Brianna's teal green eyes lock onto mine and I see the fear in them. Wide and filled with fear. But also with trust.

And that's all I need.

Audrey steps out of the shadows. "Andrew Harrington,"

she says with a scolding tone to the unidentified man. "Attorney Harrington. What are you doing?"

"Just taking what's ours," he says.

"Yours?" Audrey asks.

While Sheriff Morgan is distracted with Audrey, I move in, my brothers right there with me.

Morgan tries to use Brianna as a shield, but Bradley slips around behind him,

With a sharp yank on Morgan's shoulder, Bradley wrenches him backward, breaking his grip on Brianna.

Brianna stumbles free, falling into my arms, while Wyatt steps in to pin Morgan down.

"Told you. You should be sheriff," Wyatt tells Bradley.

"Assaulting a police officer," Morgan says. "Smart move. You're all going down."

"I don't think so," Lilah says. "I've got it all on video."

Sure enough, Lilah is holding her phone up, videotaping everything.

"Smart move," Brianna says, rubbing her neck.

"It worked against me. It'll work against him."

"You okay?" I ask Brianna.

"I am now."

Audrey, hands on her hips, is standing in front of Andrew Harrington.

"Explain yourself," she says.

Andrew blows out a breath. "It was a bad idea. I knew it was."

"Why?" Audrey persists. "Why are you doing this?"

"The house. It should go to my nephew."

"Wait," Audrey says, looking a little pale. "Your nephew?"

"That's right. My sister wouldn't do anything about it, so her brothers had to do it."

"Brothers?" Lilah asks, looking from the sheriff to the attorney. "You two?"

"That's right. This house rightfully belongs to our sister and her son. You may have been married to him, but the boy is his legacy."

"Didn't she get enough? She got everything else." Brianna finds her voice.

"She might not want it now, but she'll want it later," Andrew persists.

"Enough of this," I say. "Where's Trent?"

"I'm right here," Trent says, stepping around the curve in the trail, two state policemen right behind him. "I made some calls."

Wyatt releases the sheriff and steps aside.

"Sheriff Morgan," one of the state troopers says. "We've had our eyes on you for some time now. Looks like you finally tipped your hand."

"It's over, Morgan," the other trooper says as he slaps handcuffs on Morgan and proceeds to read him his rights.

"Thanks for your help in all this, Wyatt," the first trooper says.

"The pleasure was all mine."

As the state troopers haul Morgan and Harrison off, Bradley and I look at Wyatt.

"What was that about?" I ask. "What did you do?"

"I've been giving them copies of all the notes. Keeping them in the loop."

"You didn't say anything," Lilah says.

"I couldn't," Wyatt says. "I was working undercover."

"Undercover?" Bradley wraps his arms around Audrey.

"We're going to be needing a new sheriff," Wyatt says.

I take Brianna's hand and we all start walking back toward the house.

"Guess you've got the job," Bradley says.

"Nope. It's all you, Bro," Wyatt wraps his arms around Lilah. "All my plans revolve around this one."

"What kind of plans?" Bradley asks.

"You know. Marriage. Babies. The usual."

"Told you," Audrey says to Bradley.

"You want to get in on that?" I ask Brianna.

She elbows me. "I think you need to work on your delivery."

I grin. "All I need is a little incentive."

She stops right there, stands on her toes, and kisses me on the lips. "Consider yourself incentivized."

She looks at me with her teal blue eyes and I am indeed incentivized.

THIRTY-NINE

Brianna

AFTER A LATE DINNER, we sit in front of the fireplace with its dangerously high flames.

Audrey snuggled up next to Bradley. Lilah lying with her head on Wyatt's lap.

Me sitting pressed up next to Caleb, his arm around me.

"Are you sure you're okay?" he asks, kissing me on the top of my head.

"I'm sure. I knew you'd be there to rescue me."

"Twice in one day," I say. "I'm on a roll."

"I can't wrap my head around an attorney in Houston

and a sheriff in Whiskey Springs being brothers," Audrey says.

"I just assumed Morgan was his last name," Lilah says.

Bradley says. "I think they might be half-brothers. I never knew Morgan to have a brother."

"You would have known," Audrey says. "Since he's from here."

"You're right, my love, I would have known."

"And since you never met Audrey's attorney," I say. "You couldn't have put it together."

"I guess they'll come back tomorrow to take our statements," Lilah says, hiding a yawn behind the back of her hand.

"You can't be sleepy," I say. "With all this excitement."

"Missed her nap, didn't you, Little One?" Wyatt holds her close.

"Yes. I did."

"Creative people need their naps," Wyatt says.

Lilah looks up at him. I can see the love in her eyes. Wyatt gets her. He really gets her.

As an older sister, that makes me so happy for her.

"It's dark outside," Caleb points out.

We all look toward the windows with closed window shades.

"Do you think we'll ever feel safe enough to sit in here with them open at night again?" Audrey asks.

"I sleep with my window shades up," I say.

"You're quite the rebel."

"Just one of the many things you like about me," I say, looking up at Caleb.

"That and your brilliant mind."

"I can't figure out why they targeted Brianna," Audrey says. "I'm the one they want out of here."

"Opportunity for one," Wyatt says. "And also they know that the most efficient way to get you out of here is to threaten your family."

"What were they going to do with her?"

"I don't know."

"Nothing," I say. "I was getting ready to fight back. I just had to wait for the right moment."

They all look blankly at me. I shrug. "That and I knew someone would come looking for me. Especially with Biscuit running to the house."

"I'm getting really fond of that horse dog," Lilah says sleepily.

"He's a good dog," Bradley says.

"I'm going to get this one up to bed before she falls asleep right here," Wyatt says.

"You ready for bed?" Bradley asks Audrey.

"Yes." She whispers something to Bradley and he glances toward us.

"Good point."

They all head up to bed, leaving Caleb and me alone in front of the fire, down to a normal level now.

"It seems a shame to waste such a good fire," he says.

"You angling for a reason to stay the night again?" I ask.

"I'm getting used to sleeping here. Besides, I brought extra clothes this time."

She smiles. "Well then. I guess that settles it."

"But that's not really a good reason, is it?"

"It is if you're looking for one."

"I've got all the reason I need right here," he says, pressing his lips against mine.

I sigh and sink into the kiss.

"We're getting into dangerous territory here, you know," he murmurs against my lips.

"How so?"

"This is how it happens."

I arch forward, my lips back on his again. Even a moment apart from him is too much time away.

"I don't know what you mean."

He shifts me so that I'm leaning back against his arm.

"Boy meets girl. Boy rescues girl."

Another light kiss.

"Boy falls in love with girl."

My heart skitters and I know I'm already more than halfway in love with the boy.

"You know I'm a rebel," I say.

"Yes. You are a rebel. And yes. That's just one of the many things I love about you.

The End.

KATHRYN KALEIGH

Still Yours (Maybe)

STILL YOURS (MAYBE)

PREVIEW

Chapter 1
Hannah Moore

Friday Night Pizza

The Pizzeria with its fire-roasted sauce and wood-fired pizza is owned and run by a second-generation family of Italians. Their parents brought their recipes with them when they moved to America from Italy, making it a unique and popular restaurant in the heart of Uptown Houston.

Italian music spills from hidden speakers blending with

the sounds of the busy kitchen and the chatter of customers. Silverware and glasses clink against each other.

The tables are not those of the typical pizza parlor. The heavy tables are covered with thick white cloth tablecloths, candles in chunky white vases burning on each one.

Lush green strands of ivies wound their way up columns interspersed among the tables and over time crawled their way along the crossbeams in the ceiling, giving the indoor restaurant an almost outdoor feel.

The scent of Italian spices blends with the rich scent of pizza and the wood smoke from the oven.

"One week from today," Olivia announces with obvious fanfare, leaning forward, her chin-length blonde-streaked hair falling forward. "You'll be married. Mrs. Theodore Smith."

Ignoring a reflexive wince, I smile brightly. Pretending a big part of that brightness isn't forced, I say the first thing that pops into my head. "I'm thinking maybe I'll keep my last name."

My two friends sitting on either side of me at the table look at me with horror in their eyes. Olivia and Madison.

Olivia is the sassy one with blonde-streaked short hair to match. Sassy is a good word to describe her. I've heard her called mouthy by a couple of people over the years. The word doesn't not fit her, but sassy is better.

Madison has long straight chestnut hair, all natural. Matches her all-business way of approaching the world. Her reading glasses do nothing to hide the beauty behind them. Serious. I'd say the best word to describe Madison is serious.

And I have shoulder-length hair in a raven-dark color, according to my stylist. If I had to sum myself up in one word, I'd have to go with complicated.

Lifting my glass of Pinot Noir with hints of cocoa, blackberry, and dark plum, I take a little sip. The red wine feels needlessly indulgent, but we're celebrating.

The three of us usually come here on Saturday nights and have a cold beer with our pizza. As Olivia sort of pointed out, I won't be here next Saturday. I'll be on my honeymoon.

Sort of honeymoon. Theo and I are combining his college football coaching conference with our honeymoon. In Tampa, Florida. What kind of fiancé would I be to say no to that? A honeymoon paid for by his college?

As he put it, that's money we can put toward a house one day. Maybe the excuse falls flat for me, but I figure it's because I'm not really a beach kind of girl. There's that and then there's the fact that his days will be spent at the conference.

I'm not for certain what I'm supposed to do all day while he's conferencing, but I'm good at figuring things out. I'll probably do some work of my own.

We use the word honeymoon loosely.

The little pizzeria in Uptown Houston is crowded as it always is. Its popularity is as much about the atmosphere as it is for the food. The food, however, is nothing to complain about. Fire roasted with handmade crust. I usually get their specialty, the margarita pizza.

The pizzeria's got that upbeat, urban vibe that people, young and old are drawn to. It's also just two blocks over from the Galleria. Far enough away that the patrons are mostly locals, but close enough that being here is still part of the happening area.

The servers may not know our names, but they recognize us. Our server tonight is John, a college student with hair too long. Claims to be a business major, but I'm not buying it. When I was a business major, and not that long ago, a guy would have been called onto the carpet for not putting forth a professional image. Maybe things are different now. Or maybe he goes to a more liberal college.

Not my problem.

"Here you go," John says. "Good hot breadsticks. Fresh out of the oven."

"Can we get some marinara sauce?" Madison asks.

"It's on its way," John says, turning just in time to see a waitress coming this way with a tray. "There it is now."

He snags the cup of marinara off her tray as she keeps walking. She says something we can't hear to John.

He just shrugs and sets the cup of marinara in front of Madison. "All good?"

"All good."

With that, he disappears into the shadows.

"I don't think that was ours," I say.

"Neither do I," Olivia agrees.

"Oh well." Madison dips her breadstick into the sauce and happily takes a bite.

The bar is currently packed, as it always is on Saturday nights. There's a line to get a table, too. And another line for takeout.

"Why would you keep your own name?" Madison asks, taking a sip of her sparkling white wine.

Just because. "Smith is such a common name," I say. "And my MBA is in my maiden name." I shrug uncomfortably. Although keeping my name has more than crossed my mind since I agreed to marry Theo, I've never actually said it out loud.

Now, saying it out loud and getting such a negative reaction from my two best friends, I'm wondering if maybe something is wrong with the way I think.

"That's why I'm never getting married," Olivia declares definitively.

Now Madison and I look at her as though she's lost all logical thought.

"Does Dan know that?" I ask.

"Stan. His name is Stan." She bites into a crispy breadstick.

"Okay. Does Stan know that?"

"Stan doesn't need to know it," Olivia says with definite sass. "Because I'm never getting married."

Madison and I exchange a glance. That is most definitely Olivia logic at its best.

"Moving on," Olivia says. "Have you decided whether

you're moving into Theo's place or if he's moving into yours?"

"We're still undecided," I say. "My place is closer to my work. His is closer to his work." I shrug. "We'll figure it out."

Madison visibly shudders. "Cutting it kind of close, don't you think? I would have needed to know this like a year ago."

"We didn't even know we were getting married a year ago."

"And that's a different topic," Madison says.

I give her a pointed look. Madison doesn't do anything that isn't on her five-ten-fifteen year spreadsheet. I've seen that spreadsheet. There is no husband on it. And yet she dates. I don't quite know why she dates when she seems to have no plan for marriage. Unlike Olivia, she just doesn't come right out and state her opposition to the institution of marriage.

The three of us had met at the Arabella, an exclusive high-rise condo building, just over three years ago. I had been a cat sitter. Olivia and Madison had been dog walkers.

We'd somehow ended up on the same elevator at the same time. Olivia and Madison had both been walking dogs and I'd been holding a cat in a carrier that I'd had to take to the vet for a client.

You would have thought that the three of us would have been fierce competitors. And yet we had too much in common to not become fast friends which soon, by way of

Madison's prophetic spreadsheet, somehow morphed us into business partners.

"Are we getting the usual?" Madison asks, opening up one of the menus.

"Yes," Olivia says. "I'm up for some Hawaiian pizza."

"Hannah?"

I set my glass down. "I'm just going to have a salad."

"Since when?" Olivia asks with a vexed expression. "I thought salads were your weekday thing."

"They are," I say. "But I've got a wedding dress to fit in."

"You'll be lucky if it doesn't just drop off of you already," Madison says. "Didn't they already tuck it in once?"

"Yes," I say. "But I can't be too careful, you know."

Olivia and Madison exchange a look.

"You're losing too much weight," Olivia says. "Order a pizza. Otherwise your dress is just going to hang there like a feed sack.

"Jitters," Madison says tell Olivia. "It's normal."

"Definitely the jitters," Olivia says.

"I don't have the jitters," I say, but it's a half-hearted protest. I've got something. I just don't think it's the jitters.

A large table nearby filled with a dozen women erupts into applause as a young lady stands up. She's wearing a white sash with the word *Bride* embroidered on it.

"Ooh," Madison says. "We should get you one of those sashes. You can wear it everywhere. All week."

"No. You should not. I wouldn't wear it."

"She's no fun," Olivia says, swirling the wine in her glass.

"We already knew that," Madison says.

I'm not even listening to them anyone.

I'm watching the activity at the front door.

Two men, handsome men, just walked in. Both of them are wearing black business suits with white button-down shirts. Nothing unusual about that.

They're striking with their suits and their expensive haircuts, their handsome clean-cut features (nothing unusual about that either around here), but that's not what has snagged my attention.

I know one of them. I REALLY know him.

"Hannah," Madison says, following my gaze. "Are you okay?"

I don't answer. I can't get a word out past the lump in my throat.

The man who just walked through the door is none other than Jack Thompson.

My Jack Thompson from Alpine Falls.

My husband.

STILL YOURS (MAYBE)

PREVIEW

Chapter 2

Hannah

Of All The Pizza Joints

Jack must have felt me staring in his direction.

It's not a small restaurant and we're not sitting near the door. We're sitting somewhere in the middle and there are people all around us. Sitting. Walking. Standing around waiting for a seat at the bar.

But he sees me.

It's like our eyes meet across the crowded room. Just like in the movies.

After saying something to his friend, a man slightly older, I don't recognize, he peels away and heads right for our table.

After my first response, freezing, my second instinct is to flee. The restroom isn't far away. I can make it before he gets here.

But being frozen in place has already won out.

Jack, his gaze never leaving mine, walks right up to our table and stops next to my chair.

"Hello Hannah," he says.

Jack is wearing a charcoal business suit with Skye Travels embroidered over the jacket pocket. His dark-colored suit and white button-down shirt are a uniform.

"Jack. What are you doing here?" I clasp my hands together in my lap.

"Of all the pizza joints, we end up in the same one. What are the odds?"

"I can't even begin to fathom."

"How are you?" he asks, his glacier blue eyes sweeping over my face. "You look well."

"I'm okay."

"I'm here with a client," he says. "So I've got to get back to it." He gaze leaves mine long enough to glance around at Madison and Olivia. "Ladies." He nods.

Then he puts a hand on my shoulder. "Good to see you Hannah."

"You too." I watch him walk away. Back to his client.

"Who was that?" Madison asks, leaning forward, her eyes wide.

"I don't know," Olivia says. "But I do know one thing. That is not Theo."

I blink and turn back to my friends as though coming out of a daze. I look from one to the other.

They both have me pinned with their gazes.

"That was Jack Thompson."

"Jack..." Olivia's eyes get huge. "THAT Jack." She turns to Madison. "Hannah was married to him."

"Get out," Madison says, looking at me now. "Married? Why didn't I know this?"

"It never came up," I say.

"It never came up," Madison says with a shake of her head. "That's the kind of thing that comes up." She looks at Olivia accusingly. "You knew."

"It came up," Olivia said in my defense.

"Well," Madison says. "As one of your two maids-of-honor. The responsible one. The one also left in the dark. I should let you know that the court is going to need a copy of your divorce papers."

"Of course," I say. "Of course they do."

"And you happen to have a copy?"

I glance at Olivia, but she's no help. Her eyes are on the menu, even though I know she knows exactly what she's going to order. "Not exactly. But I can get a copy. It's not a problem."

"Good," she says with a glance over her shoulder in Jack's direction. "Definitely not Theo."

"No," I say, shoving the hair off my face. "Definitely not Theo."

"You didn't tell me," Madison says to Olivia.

"Not mine to tell," Olivia says.

Right now I'm thinking I have one friend too many. Not that I want to ditch either one of them.

But maybe both.

Maybe I need to just ditch both of them.

But in the meantime, I've got a bigger problem.

I've got to get in touch with the clerk's office in Alpine Falls and get a copy of my divorce papers.

Maybe I thought that if I didn't tell anyone, no one would know. This is Houston. That was Colorado. It was a lifetime ago and in another world.

It was so long ago, who could possibly care about it?

I must have said that last bit out loud.

"It's all online now," Madison says. "When you go to get your license in Harris county, there's a good possibility that your social will show that you were married."

"I don't know." I hold up a hand at her expression. "But I'll get it okay? I'll get it Monday."

"Does Theo know about this?"

I slowly shake my head. "I guess he's going to find out, isn't he?"

"I don't see any way around it, Honey," Madison says.

"I'm sure it'll all be okay," Olivia says, her gaze straying over to where Jack is sitting with his client.

Of course it will.

Of course it will be.

I'm getting married one week from today.

To a perfectly nice man.

Who is most certainly not Jack.

It's been ten years since I've seen Jack Thompson.

The cute boy I'd been married to is now a handsome man. One my friends don't seem to be able to stop checking out.

Can't blame them.

I'd be the same way, but I don't dare even glance over in his direction.

Not a good idea.

Not good at all.

STILL YOURS (MAYBE)

PREVIEW

Chapter 3

Jack Thompson

I'D BEEN to this Italian pizzeria once before with, actually, a different client. Very disconcerting odds since both clients, even though they don't know each other, picked the same restaurant.

That had been a few months ago, but it had not been nearly as interesting then as it is tonight.

It has the same lively urban feel to it. The same blend of Italian herbs and fire baked pizza dough filling the air.

The same Italian music mixing with the chatter of

customers and the sounds of activity coming from the kitchen.

But tonight Hannah is here. Hannah, a woman I haven't seen in ten years.

The same Hannah I think about every single day.

The same Hannah I married that summer right after high school.

"I'd offer you a glass of wine," my companion, Caleb Winslow says. "But I know you won't take it."

"Bottle to throttle," I say, forcing my attention back to Caleb.

Caleb Winslow hired me to fly him from Alpine Falls to Houston. He has a meeting in the morning. Then I'm flying him back up to Alpine Falls after lunch.

I haven't been doing much flying lately. I took some time off from my job at Skye Travels to help my dad out around the ranch.

That's one of the great things about Noah Worthington, my boss. He firmly believes in both ideals and actions that family comes before all else.

When Caleb called, I jumped at the chance to get back in the cockpit. Like all pilots, at least the ones I know, I'll take any excuse for flying that I can get.

I don't mind feeding and grooming horses. Don't mind helping my dad out with any of it. I don't even mind mending fences or chopping wood or any of the other physically intensive jobs required to keep his place going.

I even rather enjoy the guided horseback tours we

provide for tourists, taking them along the river and up into the back country, mostly for just a few hours at the time. Dad has always been the one leading the guided horseback rides, but with him temporarily out of commission, I've stepped in to do just about everything.

And if there's one thing I've learned over the past month or so, everything is a LOT. As a kid, working on the horse ranch, I'd known there was a lot of work involved, but since I hadn't been the one in charge, I hadn't known just how much all that work was.

Even though none of that's a problem for me, the sky still calls to me.

Sometimes I think about getting my own airplane so I can do both. Help out my dad with the family business and provide private flights.

Unless I can find someone willing to practically donate a small airplane, though, that's not something in my immediate timeline.

"So how's your dad?" Caleb asks after he orders a glass of wine for himself and I order a glass of sparkling water.

"He's still mending. The docs say he'll be out a couple of more months at best."

"But your mom is able to do some of the tours, right?"

"She can and she's quite good at it. The tourists love her. But she doesn't like leaving my dad alone. She's taking a tour in the morning, but she hired someone to come in to sit with him. Has a list of instructions a mile long."

"She's a dedicated lady. Dedicated to the business, but dedicated to your father even more. That's important."

"Hard to find," I say. My gaze is drawn back to where Hannah sits with her two friends.

I couldn't not speak to her.

I've been wanting... needing... to talk to her for years, but she vanished off the face of the earth as far as I could determine. Absolutely no social media presence. How she managed that these days, I'll never know. Seems like everybody puts their business out there for everyone to see in one form or another.

Truth is, though, I'm the same way. Other than my family's website, I don't do much on social media either. So I guess Hannah and I are kindred spirits in that way.

Unfortunately, she's having what looks like a business dinner, just as I am.

Can't very well talk to her about anything personal when she's with work associates or even friends.

At least now I have a better idea where to find her.

Houston.

Unfortunately I'm not going to be here long to find her, much less actually talk to her.

And now. Seeing her again. After all this time.

I want to talk to her all that much more.

But it's not going to happen on this trip.

Not only am I fairly certain I can't bear to go another ten years without seeing Hannah again, things have changed.

I have no choice now.
I have to find her.

STILL YOURS (MAYBE)

PREVIEW

Chapter 4

Hannah

Crumbling ***Options***

"IMPOSSIBLE," I say, glaring at my phone.

"Meow."

Reaching down, I pick up Bandit, a little teddy bear of a cat, technically an oversized Snowshoe with thick soft fur, and hold him close against me.

I named him Bandit because of the dark patches over

his eyes. He has chocolate colored ears and tail and white mittens on his feet. He has beautiful blue eyes and loves to talk. The love of talking is the Siamese in him.

"It'll be okay, right?" He purrs and rubs his face against my chin. "You're making it very hard for me to give you up, you know that, right?" He just purrs louder. "But I have to tell you, you smell like tuna."

Bandit is one of the cats I'm supposed to be putting on our website so he can be adopted. I've had him living with me for three weeks now and I still haven't posted his photo and info on the company website.

I'm surprised Madison hasn't said anything to me about it. I think she's giving me a break because of my upcoming wedding, but honestly, one has nothing to do with the other.

I just happen to like Bandit

I sit down on the sofa in my little living room and put on the brushing mitten he likes.

With papers scattered over my coffee table, it looks like a tornado came through my apartment.

Madison and Olivia are right about one thing. Theo and I have to figure out where we're going to live. Getting married in less than a week and neither one of us has made a move in either direction.

We both still have our leases and neither one of us has started packing. I'll be the first to admit, it is a bit unusual.

Right now, though, I have more important things to deal with.

While I brush Bandit, I sort through what I know.

The clerk's office in Alpine Falls doesn't have any record of my divorce. They have the marriage license. Of course. But no record of the divorce.

I called this morning. Then I called this afternoon. Got the same answer.

"I'm sorry, Mrs. Thompson. We don't see any record of your divorce. Do you think maybe it was filed in a different county?"

What county? Seriously. Jack and I got married in Alpine Falls. We lived in Alpine Falls. We got divorced in Alpine Falls.

But Alpine Falls has not held up its end of the bargain.

Feeling my options crumpling, I Face Time Olivia.

She's at the gym running on the treadmill.

"How do you do that?" I ask.

"Do what?"

"How do you run and talk at the same time?"

"I'm in shape?" It's a statement that comes out as a question.

"Of course you are."

"What's wrong? You look vexed."

"I am vexed."

Bandit walks across my lap, turns around and walks back.

"Is that Bandit?" Olivia asks.

"No. If Madison asks you about it. No. This is definitely not Bandit."

Olivia laughs. "Don't worry. I won't tell on you."

"Good."

"Now tell me what's wrong."

"I don't know. You're in a public place."

And I can barely hear her over the roar of the treadmill and her feet pounding on the belt.

She glances left and right. Then shakes her head. "I'm wearing a headset. No one can hear you."

"Right. Well. So I called the Alpine Falls Clerk's office to get the divorce papers."

"Okay."

"They don't have them."

"What do you mean they don't have them?"

"They have no record of our divorce." I make a concerted effort to keep my voice from going full on high-pitched panic mode.

"Did you file it somewhere else?"

"That's what they suggested. No. Actually I didn't file it at all."

"Who did?"

Who did.

An innocent enough question. One I should have an answer to.

"The attorney," I say, but I've been through every piece of paper I own and I don't have a copy of it. Shouldn't I have a copy of something important like that?

"Don't panic," Olivia says. "There has to be a way to fix this."

"I've called twice now. Talked to two different people. The only two people who work there."

"You have to go there and get it yourself."

"I can't just go there and get it."

"Of course you can. It's your divorce paper. They have to give it to you."

"I don't think it's a matter of them not wanting to give it to me. I think they can't find it."

"Sometimes in those small towns like that, you have to show up to get things done."

"How do you know that?"

Olivia slows the treadmill and starts walking. It only helps me hear her a little bit better.

"I watch television. Small towns are like that."

"Well." Bandit nips at my chin. "I can't go. I can't leave Bandit."

"That's why you're not supposed to get close to the pets you're putting up for adoption."

"Try telling that to Bandit."

"You two are too far gone." She takes a drink of water from her bottle. "I think you're going to end up keeping him."

"I can't do that. I can't have a pet in my apartment."

"Oh. Right. But... Bandit's a cat... and he's in your apartment."

"Hush now. The walls might have ears."

"What about Theo's place?"

"What about it?"

"Can he have a cat?"

"I don't know." I wince. "Theo's not really into pets."

Olivia hits stop on the treadmill and picks up her phone, bringing her face closer to the phone so I can clearly see her stunned expression. "Wait. You're marrying a man who's not into pets."

I shrug.

"He does know that pet adoptions are your career, right?"

"I'm pretty sure he knows that."

"But he doesn't like pets." Oliva runs a towel over her face. "How did I not know this?"

"I guess it never came up."

"Does Madison know this?" She starts walking again.

"It's not a big deal. Theo's okay with cats as long as they're temporary."

"Oh. Well. I guess that makes it alright then." Sarcasm drips from her words.

"Maybe you can go," I say.

Olivia glares at me. "They won't give your divorce papers to me."

"Why not? It's a matter of public record."

"No. I'll be the one keeping Bandit. You need to go. They know you there. They'll give you the papers."

"You're much more intimidating."

"That is true." Using both hands, she makes a swing at her short blonde hair. "But that's not that point. You might need to sign something."

"Sign what?"

"I don't know. Maybe you'll have to get new papers."

"I don't want to talk to you anymore."

Olivia grins. "I'll shower and be over to pick up Bandit." She jabs a finger at me. "Go online and buy a plane ticket."

"With what?" I can't help thinking about my maxed out credit card.

"Get Theo to buy it."

"Have you met Theo?" I ask.

Olivia holds up her hands. "You're the one getting married to him."

"Got to go," I say. "I have things to do."

"Sometimes the truth hurts," Olivia says before she ends the call.

I hate it when Olivia is right.

But I get on my phone and start looking for a plane ticket. The first one I can afford isn't until tomorrow and it leaves at seven a.m. In the morning.

My credit card protests, but somehow goes through.

When the receipt comes in, I see why the ticket is so affordable. It's a one-way ticket to Denver.

Dropping back onto the couch, I groan.

Bandit jumps into my lap.

I wrap my arms around him. "The worst part is I have to leave you here with Olivia."

Bandit just purrs and bites at my chin.

"I'll be back before you know it."

Maybe if I say it out loud, it will manifest and come true.

Keep Reading Still Yours (Maybe)...

DON'T MISS ANY OF THE BOOKS IN THE GRAVITY OF US SERIES:

www.kathrynkaleigh.com

Sign up for my NEWSLETTER to get all my romance releases, sales, Kickstarter announcements, and a **FREE** romance, SEALED WITH A KISS